FROM BRENTWOOD HIGH

Undercover Artists

Live! From Brentwood High

1 ▪ Risky Assignment
2 ▪ Price of Silence
3 ▪ Double Danger
4 ▪ Sarah's Dilemma
5 ▪ Undercover Artists

Undercover Artists

JUDY BAER

••••••••••••••••••••••••••••

BETHANY HOUSE PUBLISHERS
MINNEAPOLIS, MINNESOTA 55438

Published by Bethany House Publishers
A Ministry of Bethany Fellowship, Inc.
11300 Hampshire Avenue South
Minneapolis, Minnesota 55438

Printed in the United States of America.

Library of Congress Cataloging-in-Publication Data

Baer, Judy.
    Undercover artists / Judy Baer.
        p.   cm. — (Live! from Brentwood High ; book 5)
    Summary: While working on a program about
graffiti, the crew of Brentwood High's student-run
television news show learns about long history of this
phenomenon and comes to a better understanding of it.

    [1. Graffiti—Fiction. 2. High schools—Fiction.
3. Schools—Fiction. 4. Television broadcasting of
news—Fiction. 5. Christian life—Fiction.] I. Title.
II. Series: Baer, Judy. Live! from Brentwood High ;
bk. 5.
PZ7.B1395Ul   1996   96–10061
ISBN 1–55661–390–3   CIP
                                                   AC

For Babe Belzer—
Mother of the Year and
role model for us all!

JUDY BAER received a B.A. in English and Education from Concordia College in Moorhead, Minnesota. She has had over thirty novels published and is a member of the National Romance Writers of America, the Society of Children's Book Writers, and the National Federation of Press Women.

Two of her novels, *Adrienne* and *Paige*, have been prizewinning bestsellers in the Bethany House SPRINGFLOWER SERIES (for girls 12–15). Both books have been awarded first place for juvenile fiction in the National Federation of Press Women's communications contest.

LIVE

FROM BRENTWOOD HIGH

CHAPTER 1

LIVE
FROM BRENTWOOD HIGH

Avoid problems in the morning—

sleep until noon.

Shane Donahue slouched over a desk in Chaos Central, ignoring the turmoil that was churning around him. The final touches were being put on a new *Live! From Brentwood High* television show. Shane, however, seemed unaware of the work being done. Instead, he idly doodled with his pen on the top of the desk. His dark blond hair fell over his eyes, and his angular face was intense. Occasionally he would flip the hair from his eyes with a shake of his head.

As Shane worked at the drawing, his pen strokes grew more and more expansive.

Andrew Tremaine, who was seated next to him, was engaged in much the same activity. He was drawing on the back of his notebook, however, instead of the desk. His six-foot, two-inch frame was hunched over the too-small desktop, his ocean blue eyes intent on the paper in front of him.

The cover of his notebook was already full of

sketches, mostly of futuristic-looking cars. Occasionally he'd inserted a pair of obviously feminine-looking eyes or lips in the margins.

"Want a piece of paper?" Andrew asked, opening the notebook, which was also filled with his scribblings.

"Nah, this is fine. I'm just killing time until Ms. Wright needs me."

At that moment, Jake Sanders and Darby Ellison entered and moved across the room toward them. Jake was smiling at something Darby had said, his dimples flashing, his gray-green eyes sparkling. Darby's tumble of dark curls was restrained in a ponytail that bounced as she gestured.

"What's up?" Jake asked.

"Nothing, right now. We're just hanging out here waiting until they're ready for us," Shane said. "One of the cameras is down."

Jake pointed a finger toward Shane's doodling. It had become quite elaborate, something involving a volcano, the sun, moon, a few stars, and a gargoyle. "What's Ms. Wright going to say if she sees that?"

Shane shrugged his shoulders, unconcerned. "I've washed desks before and I probably will again. If that's the worst trouble I get into in here, then Ms. Wright should be happy." He drew bursts of flame from the gargoyle's nostrils.

Shane had walked a wilder path than the other students in the *Live! From Brentwood High* television class. He spent most of his time alone, much of it pumping iron in the weight room. He really didn't care what the others thought.

"You have a lot of talent," Darby said as she peered over his shoulder. "You should use your notebook instead of a desk. It's a shame to waste a good drawing."

"And a shame to break the rules," Shane said with a sly grin.

Rosie Wright was a demanding teacher. Shane knew perfectly well that if he annoyed her on the busiest day of the week, they'd all pay the price.

Julie Osborn and Kate Akima joined into the group.

"What have you done to your desk?" Kate stared in horror. The top of the desk was now almost completely covered with Shane's scribbling. Her dark, almond-shaped eyes threw daggers. "That's vandalism, you know!"

"You're going to get us all in trouble by messing around," Julie added. "You'd better clean that up."

"When did you become my conscience?" Shane responded with a lazy smile, unperturbed by the accusations. "I always thought Sarah was my conscience, not you."

Sarah, who had moved her wheelchair to an open spot nearby, turned pink at Shane's teasing. She was the only Christian in the group. Sarah took the ribbing as she always did—with a smile.

Silently Izzy Mooney bent over Shane's desk and stared at the elaborate creation. Izzy was a giant of a guy with an overgrown buzz haircut and rumpled, mismatched clothing. He was the unlikely genius at Brentwood High. Though no one would know it to look at him, his IQ was somewhere in the stratosphere. He stared at the words and drawings on Shane's desk, obviously processing something he found important.

"Doodling isn't allowed on desks. He should wash it off," Kate said indignantly. She balled her hands and put them on her hips.

"It's more than doodling, Kate," Izzy said seriously.

Kate blinked. "What do you mean?"

"What Shane has on his desk is graffiti."

"Graffiti?" Kate echoed. "You're right. And graffiti is vandalism. Have you seen the walls near the bus station? They're covered with this kind of junk. Totally ruined. I can't believe people would do that."

Everyone was so engrossed in the debate about graffiti that no one noticed their advisor, Ms. Rosie Wright, enter the room. "Shane, I want you to clean up that desk *right now.*"

Everyone spun to see Ms. Wright standing behind them. She had on an empire-waist silk dress, moccasin-like boots and large dangly earrings. She looked half amused and half angry. "Hurry up," she said sharply. "There's cleaning solution on the top shelf in the janitor's room that will take that stuff off. And I don't want you putting it back on again."

"Told you so," Jake said, slapping Shane on the back. Shane shrugged good-naturedly and slunk off to get the cleanser in the utility room.

After he left the room, Ms. Wright eyeballed the other students. "I don't want to see that again, from Shane or from any of you. If you're waiting in the media room for your turn to work on something, find ways to keep busy that aren't quite so purposeless and destructive. Got it?"

They all nodded somberly. Gary Richmond stuck his head into the media room from the television studio. "Rosie, I need to have you look at something."

"I'll be right there." Ms. Wright stalked toward the door. When she was gone, Andrew whistled.

"I'm amazed she lets Shane stay in this class," Julie Osborn said haughtily.

"He's daring," Kate added. "It doesn't seem to matter to him whether or not he gets into trouble."

"He doesn't respect authority," Josh added further.

"He doesn't have a dad around to *be* an authority," Darby suggested.

"What about his mom?" Molly asked. "Can't she control him?"

Questions about Shane rarely got anywhere because people knew so little about him. The conversation stalled anyway when Shane returned. Silently, but with a contemptuous sneer on his face, he washed the top of the desk. The elaborate drawing disappeared under a wad of brown paper towels. He was almost finished when Ms. Wright returned, carrying a newspaper.

"This is something you should take a look at," she said to Shane. "Since you're so interested in defiling public property, I thought you might want to read the story on the front page."

Shane wiped away the last traces of ink from his desk and took the paper.

"Go ahead," Ms. Wright said. "Read it out loud.

Everyone might be interested."

" 'City Council Discusses Setting Minimum Age to Buy Spray Paint,' " Shane read. " 'Due to growing problems with vandalism and graffiti painted on overpasses, viaducts, and the sides of buildings in Brentwood, the city council is considering setting a minimum age at which individuals may buy the spray paint most often used in this type of vandalism.

" 'It will be difficult to regulate, store owners say. They don't want to act as policemen over graffiti gangs. Members of the city council, however, believe that this is one solution to a growing problem. Graffiti costs the city many thousands of dollars in cleanup each year.' "

"That's the craziest thing I've ever heard," Andrew blurted. "Kids not able to buy spray paint? That's just stupid."

"How do they think that's going to help?" Josh asked. "If kids can't buy spray paint here in Brentwood, they'll go somewhere else. Besides, I can't imagine store owners refusing to make sales because they're afraid whoever buys it might be a graffiti artist."

"I agree," Jake said. "If someone wants to paint graffiti on walls, they'll find a way. Refusing to sell paint in Brentwood stores isn't going to stop it."

"I'd like to talk to the person who came up with that lame-brained idea. That's like saying we can prevent car accidents if we take all the cars off the road. Look at all the people who would be inconvenienced by such a ridiculous idea," Andrew stormed.

"Listen to yourselves," Sarah said softly. "Do you hear what you're saying?"

"What?"

"City Council is discussing a new ruling that sounds silly to you. Some of you want to know more about the graffiti. Others probably want answers as to how it can be stopped without resorting to far-fetched measures. . . ."

Josh snapped his fingers and his face lit with a broad smile. "Maybe we have something to thank Shane for. If Shane hadn't been caught scribbling on his desk, graffiti might never have come up."

"You're right," Darby said, catching Joshua's drift. "This definitely sounds like a story for *Live! From Brentwood High!*"

CHAPTER 2

LIVE

FROM BRENTWOOD HIGH

Even if you win the race,

you're still a rat.

"I didn't realize how late it had gotten," Sarah said as she rolled her wheelchair through the doors of the school.

Julie glanced at her watch. "Neither did I."

They'd been in the studio working with the "boom," or hanging microphones, lowering them and marking the studio floor for the best sound-pickup spots. The first time Jake had lowered the mike, he had not sufficiently secured it, and it had come crashing to the floor. The second time, Andrew had strung the mike cables too close to the light cables and they'd had electronic interference. The project had taken longer than any of them had planned.

"I told my mom I wouldn't be home until six, but it's too late to go to the mall now," Julie said.

"I agree," Jake said. "Does anybody have any good ideas?"

"Why don't we go to the park and toss the 'bee for

a while?" Andrew suggested. "I've got a Frisbee in my car and I feel like getting some exercise."

"Sounds like a good idea to me," Darby agreed.

"Let's meet at the bridge," Josh suggested. "There's a wide open space there that'll be perfect."

"Does anyone need a ride?" Sarah offered. "I've got my van." Sarah drove to school in a van that was customized just for her and her wheelchair. It also kept her in the middle of things, giving rides to her friends who didn't have other means of transportation.

"The girls can ride with Sarah. We'll pile into someone else's car," Josh said. "We'll see you at the park."

"I'll ride with Andrew," Molly volunteered.

Sarah pulled into a parking space near the bridge, her eyes on the field Andrew had been referring to. "It looks like we're the only ones here this afternoon."

"Good, I don't like it when the park is crowded," Kate said. "I wish we'd brought something to sit on, though. Those park benches look disgusting."

"There's a blanket in the back of my van," Sarah said. "Help yourself. There might be a pillow back there too."

"Have you been on a picnic lately?" Julie asked slyly. Sarah blushed beneath her red hair, and her eyes began to sparkle. She and Izzy had been dating. He was her first boyfriend.

"No, I haven't been on a picnic," Sarah finally said, "but I think it's a great idea."

Julie and Kate hustled out of the van and toward the guys as they came up from the other side of the park. Darby stayed behind to walk with Sarah. Sarah's van lift was automatic and could be maneuvered with the press of a couple of buttons. Julie and Kate already had Sarah's blanket spread on the ground when the other two girls arrived.

"Okay, who's got the Frisbee?" Kate looked for it under the benches.

"What's Izzy got in his hand?" Darby inquired.

Sarah burst out laughing. "That's a plastic bat and ball. He always carries them in his car in case his little sisters want to run off some energy."

Isador Eugene Mooney had twin sisters who kept him wrapped around their dainty little fingers. Izzy, who looked so big and fierce, was a marshmallow at heart.

"Molly and Andrew aren't here yet. Maybe we should get things going and start with Izzy's bat and ball," Darby suggested.

Darby, Jake, Izzy, and Sarah took on Julie, Kate, Josh, and Shane.

"You're up to bat first," Izzy coached. He pushed Sarah's wheelchair to the home plate they had made out of a flattened paper cup. Sarah lifted the lightweight bat to her shoulder.

Julie pitched, and Sarah swung furiously. The ball sailed off the tip of the bat into left field.

"Run," Izzy hollered. He grabbed the handgrips of the wheelchair and pushed her toward first base.

"Keep going, keep going," Darby yelled. "Kate

can't find the ball in the weeds. You can make it to second."

Izzy and Sarah skidded into second base just as Kate surfaced with the ball in her hand. She threw it wildly toward second, but the lightweight ball was blown off course by a gust of wind. Josh ran after it frantically.

"We can make it," Izzy muttered under his breath. With a sharp thrust, he pushed Sarah off second and headed toward third. Everyone was yelling and screaming by the time the wheels of Sarah's wheelchair touched third base. Not a second later, Josh, panting furiously, reached them.

"We made it! We made it!" Sarah clapped her hands. Izzy sank to the ground beside her. "Next time I'm going to stay at second base," he panted. "That thing is hard to push."

Sarah burst out laughing. "That's because I still had the brake on, Izzy. You didn't give me time to release it."

"You mean we could have been all the way home if those wheels had been working properly?" Izzy groaned.

"Probably."

He lay on the ground flat on his back and put his hands over his eyes. "I'm an idiot."

They were still laughing at Izzy when Andrew and Molly arrived. "What's going on?" Molly leaned over Izzy who was still lying on the ground. Her curly blond hair fell forward over her face.

"Where were you?" he glared accusingly.

"Andrew stopped to get some sodas. Is anybody

thirsty?" She dug a can out of her jacket pocket. They sat on the grass, sipping sodas and looking over the rolling bank to the river below them.

"It's pretty here, isn't it?" Darby said. "We should do this more often."

"I come here once in a while," Sarah said, "but I've never noticed *that* before." "That" was the base of the concrete bridge that spanned the river.

"The bridge has always been here," Julie said.

"Look at the tower legs. They're covered with graffiti."

Izzy scrambled to his feet to inspect the gray concrete. The others followed. It was even more obnoxious close up than from a distance. There were paintings, doodles, and all sorts of written phrases, limericks, and poetry marring the surface.

" 'Mike loves Mindy,' " Kate read out loud.

" 'Mindy loves Jason,' " Julie said.

"Over here it says, 'Mindy loves Tim.' "

"That girl sure gets around," Jake said with a laugh.

"There's other stuff too. Listen to this." Darby began to read, " 'Start the day with a smile—get it over with.' That's cheerful."

"Some of this *is* really stupid," Molly agreed. "Kids' stuff. But the artwork is actually kind of cool."

They were attracted to a strange humanlike figure whose head was falling off an extended neck and stretching toward the ground. "Whoever drew this had to be artistic," Molly observed.

"Do you think so?" Andrew gave a snort. "When I was a kid I used to get into trouble for drawing on walls. My mom never told me I was good."

"Me too," Josh said with a smile. "Every notebook I've ever owned was filled with pages of pictures. I never understood why people got so disgusted with me. Sometimes I just felt like being creative."

"You've got it right, Josh," Shane said quietly. "As far as I can tell, adults have the same problem with graffiti as Ms. Wright had with my drawing on the top of the desk at Chaos Central."

"Why wouldn't she?" Kate challenged. "It's vandalism."

"Is it? Have you ever considered that graffiti might be beautiful?"

"Beautiful?" Kate gestured toward concrete dikes on the far side of the river. "Does that look 'beautiful' to you?"

Shane shook his head. "I'm not talking about taggers. They give graffiti a bad name."

"What are taggers?" Darby was surprised by Shane's familiarity with the subject.

"Taggers are the guys who use spray paint and markers and run around putting nicknames like 'Jo-Jo was here' all over the street. I have friends that do it too. *That's* vandalism."

Everyone was looking at Shane now, curious as to what he would say next. "Taggers are scribblers who dirty up walls. Then people think all graffiti is scribbling."

"And it's not?" Izzy asked.

"Some of it is very artistic and really good."

"I don't know if I'd go that far," Jake said, "but some of the stuff *is* better than others. You can see the difference between someone who might have potential artistic ability and the ones who are just ... taggers."

"Exactly. Some of the people who put marks on these walls couldn't even afford to buy a canvas," Shane said with conviction. "Given a chance, I'll bet a few of these walls could become pieces of art."

"They are artistic, but that doesn't give graffiti artists the right to scribble on walls in public places, does it?"

"Maybe not," Shane said. "All I'm saying is that people don't *appreciate* graffiti. It isn't all easy, you know."

Everyone was staring at the concrete wall now.

"There's a pretty good picture of a couple dancing," Izzy pointed out.

"That's not bad, but this looks like a mess," Kate said. "Someone's written over one person's name with another."

"That's 'crossing out'—writing over someone's code or nickname," Shane said.

"What else do you know about this?" Izzy asked.

Shane shifted from one foot to the other, looking uncomfortable. "Why?"

"You obviously have the vocabulary," Izzy persisted. "Let us in on it."

Shane thought for a moment before speaking. "Well, you could say that this wall has been bombed." He gestured toward the thick layer of writing and pictures that had been scrawled across the surface. "When you heavily graffiti a wall, it's called 'bombing.' Sometimes that's done by a whole crew or group of graffiti writers. A crew might even do a large mural."

"So basically the taggers are really the bad guys because they just scribble. They don't try to do anything artistic," Sarah summarized.

"That's it." There was a slight smile on Shane's face. "And if you try to stop a tagger, then you're a hero."

"So even vandals have a code of ethics." Kate sounded amused.

Shane looked at her sharply. "Sure they do. For instance, I'd never approve of 'racking.'"

"What's that?"

"Shoplifting spray paint," he said quietly. "Of course, if the City Council is going to legislate the sale of paint so that kids can't buy spray paint until they're over eighteen, then that will just encourage them to get it in other ways—like shoplifting."

"You sure know a lot about graffiti and the people who do it," Izzy said. "I never realized you were so familiar with the graffiti subculture here in Brentwood."

"You actually *know* people who do this stuff?" Sarah waved her hand toward the wall. "Serious artists, I mean?"

"Sure. A couple of them."

"Do you do it yourself?" Darby hesitated.

Shane looked at her sharply. "No."

"Where did the idea of graffiti come from, anyway?"

"It's been around for a long time," Izzy interjected. "During World War II the phrase 'Kilroy was here' was written all over this country and abroad.

The name popped up in amazing places, so it couldn't have been just one Kilroy doing the writing. It's become the most famous piece of graffiti ever."

"I remember my grandpa talking about the 'Kilroy was here' graffiti he saw when he was in the war," Jake said.

"How do you happen to know so much about the history of graffiti, Izzy?" Kate questioned.

"I wanted to find out more about it after hearing the article Ms. Wright had Shane read. It got my curiosity up," Izzy answered with a smile.

"Well, what else do you know?" Sarah was getting excited about it too.

"Usually, graffiti is localized and temporary," Izzy explained patiently, "but once in a while something catches on and spreads so quickly that it can actually become known internationally. That's what happened with the Kilroy graffiti. It even continued for several years after the war was over. No one really knows how Kilroy got started. Some thought that he was probably an infantryman who got tired of hearing the air force guys brag about how great they were. When the air force sent a flight transport command to some faraway place, they'd often find the announcement that Kilroy had gotten there first."

"What's so special about that?"

"There really isn't anything so special about what the graffiti said, but what's unique about it is where it turned up. Sometimes the 'Kilroy was here' phrase turned up in really weird places—like on an atoll where an atomic bomb was being tested. Between the time the last person was supposed to have left the island and the time the bomb dropped, no military returned. It was also found on top of the torch on the Statue of Liberty, under the Arc de Triomphe, on the topmost part of the George Washington Bridge. It even turned up in the packing cases of some wild elephants sent into the United States by the Belgian government."

"You're kidding? How did Kilroy do that?"

Izzy chuckled. "Obviously Kilroy was more than one person. The first Kilroy started a trend that others picked up on."

"They used graffiti to mark their territory," Jake said. "I read that in a book somewhere."

"But it's more than that now," Shane said.

"What do you think it is?" Andrew challenged.

Shane hesitated. He was having difficulty putting his thoughts into words. It was Sarah who spoke for him.

"I think Shane means that he believes graffiti is a form of artistic expression. It's a way street kids can say what they think. Is that right?" Sarah looked expectantly at Shane.

Warring emotions played on Shane's face. Finally he nodded. "That pretty much sums it up."

"You don't think graffiti is *wrong*?" Julie was shocked.

"I don't like destruction of property," Shane hurried to answer. "All I'm saying is that some of the people who draw graffiti could be pretty good artists if they were given the chance."

"But that's the problem, isn't it? They're never going to be given a chance. They're always going to be thought of as destructive vandals, not artists," Izzy concluded.

"What time is it?" Julie asked, interrupting the flow of the conversation.

"Almost five-thirty," Jake said after a quick glance at his watch.

"We have to leave." Kate stood up. "Will someone give Julie and me a ride?" Both girls looked directly at Andrew.

"Sure, I suppose," Andrew said reluctantly.

"Can I catch a ride as far as the garage on Third and Elm?" Shane asked. "I left my motorcycle there and I'd like to pick it up on my way home."

"That old machine of yours is always in the shop," Kate complained as they walked toward Andrew's car. "Does it ever run?"

"Motorcycles are high-maintenance items," Shane said. "They're delicate machines—fine tuned."

"I have a bicycle that's a whole lot less delicate. It never breaks down. Have you considered that?" Kate asked as their voices drifted out of hearing range.

Darby, Izzy, Jake, Sarah, Josh, and Molly stared at one another and then at the scribblings on the concrete wall.

"That was pretty interesting," Molly finally said. "How do you think he knows so much about these graffiti artists, taggers, vandals, or whatever they're called?"

"Who knows?" Jake responded. "As long as I've known Shane, he's always been on the fringes of trouble. He never really seems to be in the middle of things, but he's always on the edge."

"Maybe it has something to do with growing up without a father," Darby said.

"It must be terribly hard to know you have a dad somewhere, but that he doesn't want to be with you or your mother."

"My mom got a divorce, but that doesn't mean I automatically get into trouble," Molly said in a huff.

"I think you should give Shane a little credit," Darby spoke again. "Just because he knows some of the kids who do these things doesn't mean he does it himself. Besides, something really amazing happened here today."

"What was that?" Molly looked puzzled.

"Shane talked to us more than he ever has before. He's becoming a part of us, of the *Live!* team. I think we're very lucky."

"Why?" Jake looked puzzled.

"Because if we're going to do a story on graffiti painters for *Live!* then we have the perfect resource—Shane. He can help us do a great story. Besides, I *like* him."

"Just so he doesn't get himself or us into any trouble while we're doing the research."

"What's the harm in trusting Shane?" Darby asked. "He's had a hard life. Maybe we're the first real friends he's had."

"I agree with Darby," Sarah said. "We have a chance to be Shane's friends. I think there's a really nice guy under that tough exterior."

"Oh, Sarah, you're always looking for the best in everyone," Molly said.

"You might be disappointed, you know," Izzy put

his big hand on Sarah's shoulder, "but I believe Shane Donahue is a good guy. We can learn a lot from him if he ever spills what he knows."

They left the park feeling both unsettled and uneasy. Shane was a mystery to all of them. No one could shake the feeling that Shane was a little like a stick of dynamite ready to go off at an unsuspected moment.

———

Izzy burst into the media room the next morning looking rumpled and excited.

The media room or "Chaos Central," as it was fondly called, was in its normally disruptive state. Papers and books littered every available table and counter. Posters hung three deep, dangling crookedly off the walls. Someone had attempted to repair the curtains sagging from the curtain rods by pinning them up with a series of safety pins. With a bit of macabre humor, a plant on the windowsill had been sprayed with black paint. It was amazing that the studio was intact.

The media room was usually in turmoil. No matter how often they straightened and cleaned, clutter crept back in when no one was looking.

"I have some news!" Izzy announced.

"Are you moving?" Julie teased. "Far away from here? Or have you inherited money and plan to give us all a share?"

Izzy gave her a disgusted look. "Of course not. I've been doing some reading."

No one was impressed. Izzy was *always* reading.

"I would too if I could read as fast as you," Andrew grumbled. "Someday I'm going to take a speed-reading course and see if that helps."

"Aren't you going to ask me *what* I've been reading?" Izzy demanded.

"I wasn't planning on it," Andrew said.

"All right, Izzy, what have you been reading?" Josh finally gave in.

"I went to the library last night to check out old newspapers and the public minutes of past City Council meetings."

"Why on earth would you want to do that?" Julie asked.

"Boring," Molly yawned.

"I started thinking about the graffiti writers after our conversation with Shane yesterday. Anyway, I thought I'd take a look and see what I could find. There *is* actually a graffiti artist and even a gang forming in Brentwood. Apparently, both the community and the police have been really upset. According to the City Council minutes, the vandals are ruining the beauty of our city."

"I wouldn't go so far as to say that," Julie said. "It is pretty unattractive, but who looks at the underside of bridges anyway?"

"It's not just bridges," Izzy stated. "It's also the sides of abandoned buildings, alleys, and now store fronts too."

"What's your point?"

"For the city to take graffiti off public buildings, it is very, very expensive."

"I never thought about that," Josh said, frowning.

"The city of Brentwood has spent thousands of dollars cleaning up graffiti. Nationwide five billion dollars is spent to remove it."

Josh whistled. "Wow! Five billion, are you sure?"

"That's what the paper said. Do you guys realize how *big* this is? Most of the graffiti artists are kids our age.

"We've got to do this story, that's all I can say," Izzy enthused. "It's relevant—sort of media communications for teenagers. Plus, it's an expensive, destructive form of vandalism."

Before Josh could respond, the loudspeaker brought them to attention.

"Ms. Rosie Wright, would you please come to the office? Ms. Wright to the office."

Ms. Wright, who had been at her desk reading a script, glanced up, annoyed. As she walked out the door, Gary Richmond entered. Gary was a professional cameraman who worked with his friend Rosie on the student-run cable television channel.

His jawline was shadowed by stubble and his cap was worn backward, as usual. Gary always dressed in faded jeans and a nondescript jacket with many pockets to hold his camera paraphernalia. With his ponytail and earring, Gary looked like an unlikely instructor, but he was one of the finest. He glanced over the students in the room and settled his gaze on Izzy.

"What's got you excited this morning, Izz-man?"

"I'm telling these guys what I learned last night." Izzy went on to explain about the graffiti in the park and the information he'd gleaned from old newspapers and City Council minutes at the library.

Gary gave a low whistle. "I think maybe you're right. There may be a story here—a good one. Have you talked to Rosie about this yet?"

"If we're going to do it," Darby added, "we should track down some graffiti artists and interview them. We're also going to have to interview City Council members, maybe even the mayor. We want two sides of this picture."

"Good, very good," Izzy nodded. "And they sound like people who are going to have a hard time agreeing. Some sparks might fly."

"You think so?" Andrew looked interested. "That would be fun."

"Let's go to the park tonight and snap some pictures." Gary's excitement grew. "I remember my uncle talking about the 'Kilroy was here' graffiti during the war. Maybe it's time a new generation heard about graffiti!"

CHAPTER 3

LIVE

FROM BRENTWOOD HIGH

People who write on walls are idiots.

* * *

Speak for yourself!

Rosie Wright returned from the administration offices and walked silently toward her desk. She looked unusually serious as she sat down. Her forehead was deeply furrowed, and she chewed thoughtfully on one corner of her pen. Her bright yellow T-shirt looked out of place with her somber expression.

"Is anything wrong?" Sarah was the first to voice her concern.

"What? Oh . . . no. But thanks for asking."

"You sure *look* like something is wrong," Izzy persisted.

Ms. Wright watched the students gather around her desk. She sighed deeply and ran her fingers through her long hair. "Well, maybe something is wrong. No, not wrong, exactly, just surprising."

"What happened? Is someone sick?" The kids crowded closer.

"I just received a call from a friend of mine who's an administrator at an educational facility near here. He wants me to teach a class."

"At another school? You're not going to leave us, are you?" Kate was genuinely alarmed.

"Of course not. I've no intention of leaving Brentwood High. My friend has asked me to teach a class at the Last Chance Ranch."

Shane, the only student who had not come to the desk to gather around Ms. Wright, looked up from his computer screen with a flicker of interest in his eyes. "The Last Chance Ranch?" he echoed.

"Yes. My friend has been an administrator there for almost two years. This is the first time he's asked me to take part in his program."

Shane sauntered over to her desk to join the others. His unexpected interest was almost as surprising as the expression on Ms. Wright's face.

"I don't get it," Julie complained. "If you're going to teach a class and you're not going to another school, where are you going?"

"What *is* the Last Chance Ranch?" Molly asked quickly.

"The Last Chance Ranch is a boys' correctional facility that's considered to be just one step away from the juvenile prison system."

"I've never even heard of it before," Jake said.

Their curiosity was obvious.

Ms. Wright smiled slightly. "That's probably a good thing, Jake. The boys who *do* know about the Last Chance Ranch are usually in quite a bit of trouble with the law."

"Did you know about this before now?" Julie began to take a poll of everyone in the room. "Izzy, did you?"

Izzy shook his head. So did Josh and Andrew.

When Julie turned toward Shane, she paused. "But *you've* heard of the Last Chance Ranch, haven't you?"

Shane lifted one shoulder in a half shrug. "I have a couple buddies who have been out there," he said quietly.

Somehow, that didn't surprise anyone.

"Tell us more about this place, Ms. Wright," Sarah said. "It sounds very interesting."

"Sad to say, but the juvenile court system is becoming flooded with kids who are becoming more and more violent. The amount of crime is going up. The ranch is a last resort for delinquent youths before they enter our state prison system. Many of the boys at the ranch have been arrested for arson, car theft, forgery, or much worse. The Youth Authority in our state uses the Last Chance Ranch as a final effort to keep these kids out of the prison system."

"Sounds like a rough crowd up there," Josh observed.

"It is, indeed," Ms. Wright agreed. "Some of the kids housed there are incarcerated for murder."

"And they asked you to teach out there?" Julie looked concerned. "Is that safe?"

"Oh, I think so. The students are well supervised. Teachers from the area are often called on to teach special seminars at the Last Chance Ranch."

"Do you know much about this place, Ms. Wright?" Shane asked.

"Not much more than I've told you, Shane. Why?"

"Did you know that the ranch just placed a 're-lease' student here at Brentwood High?"

"Really? How interesting. Is he a friend of yours?"

Shane's eyes grew hooded. "A friend of a friend. I don't know him personally."

"I see."

The group looked at one another questioningly. Again, Shane had managed to surprise them.

"Who is he?"

"Is he in any of our classes?"

"Have you met him?"

Shane muttered ambiguous responses to all of their questions. Finally, they turned back to Ms. Wright.

"What's it like out there?" Molly asked. "Is it like school or like prison . . . or both?"

"From what I've gathered, life at the Last Chance Ranch is very structured, with drills, armylike routine, and uniforms."

"You're kidding! What's all that for?" Izzy looked puzzled. Everyone knew he was thinking about the uniforms. Izzy was a free-form dresser if there ever was one.

"Those things teach structure and discipline, Isador," Ms. Wright told him. "Structure and discipline are usually missing from the lives of the boys who end up at the Last Chance Ranch. They often come from single-parent homes. Many times those homes are also below the poverty level. To someone whose life is in disarray, structure is a very important thing.

"According to my friend, they run the ranch much like a military operation. The boys have to shave, shower, and do their chores before they can file to breakfast in the morning. There are school and work details as well. Because so many have gang affiliations, the administrators have found it better if all the boys dress exactly the same. They cut their hair in the same style too." Ms. Wright looked at Izzy with a smile. "Much like yours, I believe."

Izzy ran his fingers through his overgrown buzz cut. "Cool. At least those guys have got something right."

"So what happens if they refuse to listen or do what they're told?" Molly questioned. "What kind of punishment do they have for a guy who is already practically in jail?"

"When a student is 'docked' for an infraction, a day is added to the end of his sentence," Ms. Wright replied.

"They could make him stay longer and longer? Wow, that's good motivation for behaving yourself, isn't it?" Darby observed.

"I'd like to meet that new student you talked about, Shane. I wonder why he was at the Last Chance Ranch. Arson, maybe, or car theft?" Julie guessed.

"Vandalism, I bet. Probably forgery. That's pretty common these days," Andrew speculated.

Izzy was thoughtful as the others speculated on this new student. Finally he spoke. "I wonder if anyone ends up at the Last Chance Ranch for graffiti writing?"

Izzy turned to Ms. Wright. "We've been doing a lot of talking about graffiti lately, Ms. Wright. We all think it would be a great story idea. Maybe something like that could be tied into a story about the Last Chance Ranch, especially now that there's a student here at Brentwood High who's been at that facility."

"I like your idea. In fact, Izzy, I think you should go with it. Darby, Jake, you're not working on any special stories now, are you?"

They both shook their heads.

"Then, I'll assign you to this story as well. Is there anyone else who's interested in working on this?"

Shane raised his hand.

"Why do *you* want to bother with this story?" Andrew asked. "It sounds like a lot of work to me."

"I've had friends at the Last Chance Ranch," Shane said softly. "This might be a good way to learn more about it." His mouth twisted into a humorless smile. "From the outside, that is. I don't want to find out about it from the inside."

This desk is dedicated to those who died

waiting for the bell to ring.

"This place is packed. We're never going to find a table." Julie stood in the lunchroom doorway and glared at the tables filled with students.

"The lunchroom is always crowded by the time the *Live!* crew gets here," Jake retorted.

"That's because we're always getting held up in the studio," Andrew reminded them, his gaze pointed directly at Julie. "And if you were faster at the work you had to do, this wouldn't happen. I *told* you to be careful striking those booms. You aren't supposed to drop them or the cable connections."

"How was I supposed to know how hard it was going to be to take them down? I've never done it before. Besides, you're the one who smacked into the microphone with a ladder. You could have wrecked everything."

"We're going to have to start coming earlier," Darby pointed out, hoping Julie and Jake would quit complaining.

"All the fruit cups are gone again," Julie whined. "I'm getting sick of spending so much time in the media room that I miss the best food."

"Will you two break it up?" Andrew came up behind them. "You don't need a fruit cup. Eat a taco."

"All that grease. Oooh." Julie wrinkled her nose and scurried away from Andrew.

Molly, who had not seen him stop to talk to the others, ran into Andrew and nearly knocked the food off his tray. "Watch out where you're going!" she cried.

"Me?" Andrew yelped. "I was standing still. Watch where *you're* going."

Izzy came through the line, pushing Sarah's wheelchair. She held a tray of food for both of them.

"We probably won't all be able to sit together," Darby commented.

"Maybe that's best." Jake grabbed two cartons of milk. "As grumpy as everyone is today, I don't know if we *want* to sit with them."

"There's a spot over there." Josh pointed a finger toward the far corner of the room. One lonely figure sat at the end of the table.

"That's weird," Jake said. "Why haven't people filled that table?"

"Maybe that guy didn't use his deodorant this morning," Andrew smirked.

"Very funny. Have I told you what I think of your sense of humor lately?"

"Thanks, but no thanks, Molly. Let's get going or someone will take that table too."

Andrew led the way. Molly, Kate, Julie, Jake, and

Darby trailed after. Izzy and Sarah brought up the rear.

"Where's Shane?" Sarah asked.

Izzy tipped his head in the direction of the cafeteria doorway. "We've been researching for the assignments Ms. Wright gave us on graffiti and the Last Chance Ranch. He's doing stuff on CD-Rom before he eats."

"He's pretty enthusiastic, isn't he?"

"It's great. He'll be a lot of help. Shane's a really smart guy when he applies himself," Izzy said. "I'm going to like working with him on this."

Andrew, who was leading the way, sat down at the end of the long table and greeted its single occupant. "Do you mind if we join you?"

Without waiting for an answer, the others descended upon the benches.

"He doesn't look very friendly," Julie whispered to Kate as the guy shrank back and glared at them, as if by doing so, he could make them disappear.

Andrew paid no attention. He could be plenty obnoxious himself when he wanted to be, and the scowl didn't intimidate him in the least.

Darby studied the young man at the table. His hair, dark brown in color, had been shaved very close to his head. The boy had high cheekbones and narrow gray eyes. His facial features were tense and glowering. He was athletic in build, tough and rugged looking. The expression on his face darkened as he was invaded by the noisy group.

Darby could see the fury mounting in his face. With a shock, it occurred to her that he had been *in-*

tentionally scaring people away from this table. He wanted to be alone. From the daggered looks he was shooting at them, Darby understood how he had managed it.

Andrew, who was never given to observing others closely, did not seem to notice.

Izzy, however, could read people like a book. "Hi!" he said cheerfully, unloading his and Sarah's food from the tray. "I hope you don't mind if we join you. It's pretty crowded in here today."

The stranger lowered his gaze and shrugged. Hardly a welcoming gesture.

"We're part of the *Live! From Brentwood High* program," Izzy explained, determined to strike up a conversation. "Are you familiar with that?"

"No."

"It's a student-run cable television station," Izzy explained. "There's also a radio station and printing equipment we use, but television is our main area of interest. We do stories from start to finish. Research, interviews, taping, editing ... everything. Technical stuff too. Have you thought of signing up for the program?"

"Don't know anything about it. Just got here."

Izzy latched on to that bit of information—he had started this and he was determined to see it through to the end. He was going to have a conversation with this stranger whether the guy wanted it or not. "That's why I haven't seen you before. You're new, huh?"

"Sort of."

"Did you grow up here?"

The outsider muttered the name of a town about thirty miles away.

Izzy looked up. "I've been to Braddington. We interviewed someone from your high school. He was an emergency medical technician working for the local ambulance service. Do you remember Grady—"

"Don't know him," the boy interrupted sharply.

"Oh, too bad. He's a great guy."

This was as sullen and reluctant a specimen as Izzy or any of the others had ever seen. It was a tribute to Izzy's perseverance that he didn't give up.

"You went to school in Braddington before you came here?"

"No. That's just the place I used to live." It was obviously a touchy subject.

Izzy changed tactics.

"My name is Izzy. Actually, it's Isador Mooney, but my friends call me Izzy. What's your name?"

It would have been the height of rudeness if the young man had not responded. Still it sounded as if he were reluctantly dragging the name from the depth of his soul.

"Jason."

"Hi, Jason. What's your last name?"

"Danier."

"Glad to meet you. Welcome to Brentwood High. I hope you like it here."

"Right," Jason said with a snarl.

"Don't worry, it's not so bad. Some of the teachers are terrific. Rosie Wright, in our television production class, is top notch."

"Teachers and 'top notch' don't go together," Jason informed him.

The whole group was silent now. They were all eavesdropping on the conversation between the two guys.

"You must have had some lousy teachers wherever you went to school for you to think like that," Izzy said.

"Maybe they weren't all lousy, but I didn't like school much."

"You'll like it better here," Izzy assured him. "Where did you say you went to school?"

Jason looked at Izzy while weighing the question. "You really want to know?"

Izzy blinked, puzzled. "Of course, I wouldn't have asked if I didn't."

"I just transferred here from the Last Chance Ranch." Jason's shoulders squared and he looked defiant, daring Izzy to say something negative.

The expression on Jason's face was incredulous when Izzy gave a small whoop of delight.

"No kidding? This is great! We were just talking about you. Hey, guys, this is Jason from the Last Chance Ranch!"

Jason was startled by Izzy's response. What he'd meant to use as a weapon to drive Izzy and his friends away had succeeded in doing just the opposite. Jason withdrew further into his sullen shell.

"I mean it," Izzy said enthusiastically. "We're going to do a story about the Last Chance Ranch. I'd love to talk to you about it."

"It's a place I want to forget," Jason said bitterly.

"Why would I want to talk to you about it?"

"I'm sorry. I didn't mean . . ."

"Forget it. I just don't want to talk about it, all right?" He made it perfectly clear that he would be uncooperative.

Even irrepressible Izzy had to back off. He turned to Sarah instead. "I found the greatest stuff when we were researching graffiti this morning."

Sarah responded enthusiastically, "What did you find?"

"Graffiti is one of the ways that historians are able to track the developments, trends, and attitudes in our history."

"How far back does it go?" Sarah's interest was building.

"There are still writings left from early Roman times, before the birth of Christ. When my dad was younger, he traveled in Europe while in the military. One of the places he went was Rome. Do you know that in the tunnels of ancient Rome there is a place called the 'Graffiti Wall'?"

"I thought graffiti was new, that it came out with gangs," Molly said.

"It's not new at all. My dad said you can still see the etchings of ancient Romans. There are bits of humor and wisdom that they wanted to pass on to others. Sort of like a blackboard for sending messages in a public place. Cool, huh? According to the stuff I read this morning, graffiti is a form of—"

"Wall gossip," Jake interjected.

Izzy snapped his fingers. "Exactly right. That was their way of talking to one another about important—

and not so important—things."

"Like the graffiti in rest rooms," Kate said. "Most of it is stupid, and some of it's gross and perverted."

"That's because the people who are writing are in total privacy and more apt to write down their 'lowest' thoughts there."

"Seems fitting, doesn't it?" Jake said with a laugh.

"Sometimes you see graffiti that's really aggressive. People often turn to graffiti when they're frustrated or feeling helpless because they can't do anything about powers that are bigger or stronger than they are, like the government or their employer. Sometimes it can be a way to fight off pain."

"I'm not so sure about this," Josh said. He'd been quiet until now. "I think people who write graffiti aren't doing it for a noble cause. People scribble on walls or on desks," and he shot Shane a sharp glance as he joined their group, "because they're bored."

"I agree with Josh," Andrew said. "When you sit in the bathroom with nothing but a blank wall in front of you and a pen handy, why not draw?"

"Andrew, you don't actually *do* that, do you?" Molly said.

"No, of course not." Andrew first looked indignant, then repentant. "Well, I did once, but I was a lot younger then."

Even Jason was interested now. "*This* is the kind of thing you research for your television show?" He asked the question cautiously, but with a note of curiosity in his voice.

"Sure. It's great," Izzy responded. "We figure that

anything that catches *our* interest will interest all the kids at Brentwood High."

"I didn't know schools had anything like this," Jason admitted. "I might have been more interested in school if I'd known."

"Live! From Brentwood High is the best thing I've ever done," Molly said enthusiastically. "I've always wanted to be a model or an actress, but since working with Ms. Wright, I've decided that I might want to be a broadcast journalist instead."

"What kind of things have you covered?"

"Our very first story was about a teenage emergency medical technician."

Andrew, Darby, and Jake all smiled widely. "When we went to do one of the interviews, we ended up being present at the birth of a baby."

"Wow!" Jason's eyes grew round.

"And then we did a show on sexual harassment," Darby added. "And another about teenagers who are handicapped." Sarah tapped the arm of her wheelchair. "Like me."

"And you're going to do one on graffiti?" Jason asked.

"And the Last Chance Ranch," Izzy said.

"Are you planning to do the story on the negative aspects of graffiti, or the positive ones?"

Kate looked startled by Jason's question. "The negative ones, of course. There aren't any positive ones." She paused. "Are there?"

"There's *got* to be something positive about it," Josh said. "Nothing is ever totally bad or totally good. The world just isn't that black-and-white."

"Well, I can't see anything good about graffiti," Kate said huffily. "It messes up walls, it ruins people's property, and it's ugly."

"Not all of it," Jason said quietly.

"I've never seen graffiti that isn't ugly," Andrew said.

"Then maybe you haven't been in the right places," Jason countered.

"If you like graffiti so much, give me an example of something positive about it," Andrew demanded.

"He sounds like Shane," Julie muttered under her breath.

"Have you ever considered graffiti as art?" Jason challenged.

"Anyone can buy a can of black paint and wreck a wall," Andrew sneered. "That's not art."

"Then you haven't been looking at the right graffiti. Have you seen the east end of the old warehouse on Market Street?"

Andrew shook his head, but Jake snapped his fingers, a flash of recognition shimmering on his face.

"I have. There's a huge mural down there. Street art. It's great. Whoever did it had some real talent."

"That's graffiti too," Jason pointed out, "but it's by a graffiti *artist*, not a vandal."

"They're the same thing," Kate said huffily. "I don't know how you can think any differently."

Jake's face furrowed in thought. "I don't approve of painting on the sides of buildings, but Jason has a point. Someone with real talent put that drawing on the wall. It's too bad it couldn't be on a canvas where it wouldn't deface public property."

Darby was scrutinizing Jason. "How do you know so much about this, anyway?"

Jason shrugged. "I just ran into some graffiti artists, that's all."

"Did you meet them at the Last Chance Ranch?" Kate asked. "If you did, then they were vandals, not artists."

Jason shook his head adamantly. "I don't agree with you. There's a whole . . . code . . . about it."

"What do you mean?"

"Graffiti artists think of themselves as cool, mysterious people. They don't want to show their identity to outsiders. What they have to say is written or painted on walls instead."

" 'Outsiders,' meaning parents, I suppose," Julie said.

"What's new about that?" Kate retorted.

"In cities, the graffiti writers hang in groups."

"How do they find each other?" Darby asked.

" 'Writers' corners,' " Jason said. "Locations are spread by word of mouth. The graffiti writers gather there to compare their work, and," he added a little shamefacedly, "to talk about ways to avoid the police."

"I thought so," Kate said. "Criminals!"

"People just trying to express themselves," Jason retorted.

"And how do they get their paint? Steal it?" Kate was getting agitated now.

Jason cast his eyes downward.

"I thought so." Kate crossed her arms and shook her head.

Andrew looked grim. "It's going to be difficult to convince me there's anything artistic about that."

"You sure know a great deal about the graffiti subculture history," Izzy observed. "Any of it from ... personal experience?"

Jason studied everyone in the group, calculating before he responded. "I've tried it a time or two," he admitted finally.

At that moment the bell rang, signaling the end of their lunch hour. Izzy started to walk toward the door, then impulsively turned around and came back. "Jason, why don't you come to the *Live! From Brentwood High* studio after school and take a look around?"

A cautious smile lurked at the corner of Jason's lips. "Thanks, I just might do that."

CHAPTER **5**

LIVE
FROM BRENTWOOD HIGH

If I have something to say and no one listens,

I write it down.

Once school was dismissed, everyone drifted into the media room. It had become a favorite hangout for the *Live!* crew.

Izzy was busy at the computer, "surfing the net," looking for more information about graffiti. He had books from the library spread out around him. Darby and Molly had claimed a stack of magazines through which they were sorting for information on juvenile detention facilities.

"It was pretty cool talking to that Jason guy today, wasn't it?" Molly admitted.

"He seems all right," Darby said.

"Too cool, if you ask me," Andrew put in. "I don't trust him."

"Oh, Andrew, that's just because you know where he came from."

"Maybe. Any guy that thinks graffiti on walls is okay doesn't get a very high rating in my book."

"I'd like to talk more with him about it," Jake said. "I wonder if he'll stop by after school today."

"Are you kidding? I doubt we'll ever see him again." Kate wasn't working. Instead, she was sitting on the edge of the table combing her black hair and peering occasionally into a small hand mirror she'd taken from her purse.

"I think he might come." Izzy, who'd been diligently punching keys on the computer, looked up. He had the uncanny ability to do many things at once. Surfing the net and eavesdropping on a conversation was nothing to him. "Ask Shane. He talked to Jason after the rest of us went back to class."

"Where *is* Shane?" Darby asked.

"He's in Editing Bay B."

"Don't bother," Andrew said. "Jason's not coming. He's not going to last at Brentwood High."

"Why shouldn't he?" Darby protested. "Just because he was at the Last Chance Ranch doesn't mean he can't change."

"I agree with Darby," Sarah said. "We have to hope for the best, that's all."

"You're much too optimistic," Julie said. "He won't last around here. Two weeks, tops."

"I give him five weeks," Kate said. "He'll probably be on good behavior for a while before he starts goofing off again. You watch and see."

"Does somebody want to help me?" Jake asked. "We're doing a short piece on the dance troupe that's visiting tomorrow. I want to set up some silhouette lighting for the dancers to move in. It will be a great dramatic effect."

"How does it work?" Molly inquired.

"I'll light the background, and the dancing figures in front will remain unlighted. That way the figures of the dancers will be emphasized. Cool, huh?"

"I'll help you. I'd like to learn how to do that," Molly volunteered

"Izzy are you ever going to be done on that computer? I want to use it," Kate asked.

"Find another one," Izzy said without turning around. "I've found some really good stuff. I'm gonna print it out in a couple of minutes."

"Computer hog," Kate growled. "It's getting late and I have to get home sometime."

At that moment the door to the media room flew open. It made a sharp thudding sound against the wall. Jason stood framed in the doorway.

"There you are," Izzy said with obvious delight in his voice. "I was waiting for you. Come take a look at the great stuff I found on the Internet. Did you guys have computers down at the Last Chance Ranch?"

Jason did not speak. He looked sullen and even more surly than he had at noon. What's more, he was completely uncommunicative. He stalked to the computer and stared over Izzy's shoulder without speaking.

"Why is he here?" Kate whispered to Darby and Molly. "What's the use in coming if you aren't going to speak to anyone or even look around?"

Sarah put her fingers to her lips. "Shhh. He'll talk when he's ready."

The atmosphere in Chaos Central changed dramatically with Jason's appearance. Everyone began to tiptoe around and whisper quietly. It was as though Jason were a bomb waiting to go off, and no one wanted to ignite the fuse.

The printer on Izzy's computer began to hum and whir as it printed out the material he'd gathered off the Internet. With a sigh, Izzy leaned back in the chair and propped his head in his cupped hands. "There, I've got it. We've got some great info here. I think you'll be interested too, Jason."

Still Jason said nothing.

Izzy and Jake exchanged a meaningful glance.

Izzy stood up. "Would you like to take a little tour around the media room and studio?" he asked.

Jason shrugged.

"I'll show you around. Sarah, do you want to come with us?" Izzy looked pointedly at her. It was obvious he didn't want to be alone with Jason if the guy was not going to speak. Sarah moved her wheelchair toward the studio. The three of them disappeared and the door closed behind them.

"What's wrong with him?" Julie said with sneer. "He's weird. Why did he bother to come if he's not going to talk to anyone?"

"It was probably hard for him to come," Darby pointed out. "Maybe he's shy."

"He's practically been in prison. I don't think I would worry about his feelings at all."

"Maybe he wants to be friendly, but just doesn't know how," Darby suggested.

"He'd better learn in a hurry, then," Kate retorted, "because he's not going to get along at Brentwood High if he behaves like this around other people."

———

In the studio, Izzy and Sarah were struggling with Jason's uncommunicativeness. They led him through the open editing bay, the sound room, and the studio, explaining in detail every piece of equipment. Izzy spent nearly five minutes extolling the virtures of the "toaster," the technical marvel that allowed them to manipulate the images on the screen.

Jason had no questions for them, but his eyes darted from side to side as he took everything in. Still Izzy and Sarah remained cheerful, talking together to fill Jason's silence.

When Sarah, Izzy, and Jason emerged from the studio, everyone in Chaos Central lifted their heads to stare at them. Jason glared back.

Izzy rolled Sarah up to the table where several others were working. Then he pulled out two chairs, one for himself and one for Jason. He tipped his head to indicate that Jason should sit down.

Jason looked as though what he really wanted to do was turn and run the other way, but instead he sat down slowly. Izzy put his feet on the table, tipped his chair back until it was resting on only two legs, cupped his hands behind his neck, and stared at Jason.

"I have a question to ask you, if you don't mind?"

"Depends," Jason said cautiously.

"Darby, Shane, Jake, and I are working on the story about the Last Chance Ranch. Would you be willing to let one of us interview you about the place?"

Jason flushed.

Izzy held up his hand. "Please hear me out. We don't have to use your real name or a picture of you. No one has to know that you're the one being interviewed."

"For television? How's that supposed to work?" Jason sneered.

"We can block out your face or put it in shadow and distort your voice. It's easy. We do it all the time. You'd be terrific to interview. You've lived at the Last Chance Ranch. It would be a great opportunity for us if you'd be willing to do it."

Jason shook his head adamantly. "All I've wanted for the last ten months is get out of that place. Why would I want to discuss it with you or anyone, especially on TV?" His eyes darkened. "I should never have told you I came from there. When word gets around, everyone will be staring at me, wondering what kind of a freak I am."

Izzy snapped his fingers, and everyone's head came up. "Jason has a problem with confidentiality," he said briskly. "I want to put you on notice here and now that any conversations we have with him are private, personal, and not to be discussed with anyone else at school. Got it?"

Then he turned to Julie and Kate. "And if I hear from anyone that you've been gossiping about what goes on in here with our interviews, I'll deal with you myself. You'll be begging for Ms. Wright to discipline you."

Julie turned to Jason. "Even though Izzy doesn't seem to trust us, we *do* have some scruples, you know.

If we can interview you, we will consider everything you say off the record until we've cleared it with you."

Jason couldn't sit in his chair. He jumped from his seat and prowled the perimeter of the room like a caged wild animal. He touched the dried-up plant on the windowsill, the chalk in the tray beneath the chalkboard, the top of the computer screen, the edge of a chair.

"I don't know," he said finally. "When I was still at the Last Chance Ranch, I thought that once I got out I could start over. Everything would be new—a clean slate, a fresh start. But as soon as I got here I realized how different I was from the people in this school. Nobody understands me. No one even has a clue."

Jason glanced at Izzy. "I guess that's why I told you I came from Last Chance. I realized there was no use hiding it. I'm too different to fit in anyway. It's not going to work."

Jake, who had been sitting quietly in the corner, cleared his throat. "I think it's time to start wrapping things up here, guys," he said softly. "If Jason has any questions about this program or an interview, he probably doesn't feel like discussing them in front of an audience."

One at a time, Julie, Kate, Andrew, Josh, and Molly found reasons to finish up whatever they were doing and leave the room. Only Izzy, Sarah, Shane, Jake, and Darby were left.

Jake smiled at Jason. "Better?" he asked.

"You didn't have to kick them out. I haven't got anything to say. Nothing worthwhile, anyway. People who never visited the Last Chance Ranch think it's a bunch of hoodlums running wild, having to be locked in cells all day and all night. It wasn't that way. Sometimes we even forgot that we weren't just normal guys, seventeen-year-olds hanging out together."

"What *was* it like?" Darby ventured. "Can you tell us?"

"If I had to describe it," Jason said, "I'd say it was a lot like being in the army. You're up every day at six-thirty A.M. Saturdays and Sundays included. No one gets to sleep in for any reason unless you're in the infirmary. At first I thought I was going to hate it, but it's not so bad because lights had to be out at ten. Before I went to the Last Chance Ranch, I usually didn't come home until two or three in the morning, and then I always wanted to sleep until noon. Now I get up early and I go to bed early. It's okay, I guess."

"Then what?" Darby asked.

"Shower, shave, get dressed. We all wore uniforms so it didn't take long to dress in the morning. Once we'd dressed we made our beds and waited until everyone was ready before we filed out to breakfast. After breakfast we went to school. There was one teacher for every three or four guys in most classes, so actually we got a lot more attention than you do here at Brentwood. Of course, some of the guys were way behind. It took extra time for the teacher to help them catch up. School isn't hard for me so I never fell behind, even when I was doing a lot of skipping."

"Do you go to school all day?" Jake asked.

"No. Just until noon. Then we'd have lunch. After lunch we went to our jobs."

"You had a job too?"

"Sure. We all worked on the ranch. There are big gardens, and the cooks use the produce. In the summer there are always vegetables to weed. There are also lots of animals. We'd milk cows and goats, and look after the riding horses. If there was one thing I really liked about the ranch, it was the horses. We all had riding lessons, but it was also our responsibility to clean the stalls and to groom and feed the animals. Everything at the Last Chance Ranch revolves around work. No one got to hang around and do nothing, not even for a minute."

Jason appeared to be remembering something. "There's a poster in the dining hall that says 'A lazy man sleeps soundly—and he goes hungry.'"

"Proverbs 19:15," Sarah said with a chuckle. "So you worked every day until suppertime?"

"Not quite. Throughout the afternoon and evening we also had to attend counseling sessions," Jason said.

"What kind of counseling?" Jake asked. "You don't have to tell us if you think it's too personal."

"Any kind of counseling the guys needed. Over half of them had used drugs, so they had to go to Narcotics Anonymous. The rest seemed to end up at Alcoholics Anonymous. Everyone there is messed up one way or another or they wouldn't be at the Last Chance Ranch. Group therapy was usually full too. Counselors came and went all the time. They taught anger management, self-esteem building, and all sorts of trendy pop psychology stuff."

"Did you go to any of those?" Darby asked hesitantly. Jason looked down at the floor, and at first Darby thought he was going to refuse to answer.

"Group therapy sometimes, and esteem building and Bible study." He said the last so quickly it was hard to understand.

"Did you say Bible study?" Sarah asked. "A Bible study at the Last Chance Ranch?"

"It was a big deal there," he admitted. "Even though the ranch is used by the state prison system, it's funded by a private group that requests that all the inmates go to church."

"And how was that?" Sarah asked softly.

Jason considered her question for a long time. "Okay, I guess. I didn't mind. At first I thought what they were saying was pretty off-the-wall. All this stuff about 'Jesus loves you' and 'Christ died for your sins,' but," and he smiled sheepishly, "I finally kind of got to liking it." Then his eyes narrowed. "You aren't going to tell anyone that, are you?"

"Everything here is off the record, remember?" Seeing Jason's unease, Izzy changed the subject. "You really know a lot about graffiti art. Did you do much of it yourself?"

"Like I said, a few times. It's just not as bad as you seem to think it is. I can't understand why people don't get it."

"Whatever it is," Izzy pointed out, "it's pretty expensive. The United States spends about five billion dollars a year to remove graffiti—"

"I know, I know. I've heard all those lectures. Maybe it is vandalism to some people, but it can be more than that." There was a pleading note in his voice. He seemed desperate to make them understand.

"What more can it be?" Sarah asked softly.

"A way for someone to express himself. To let people know what he's thinking." Jason's gaze lowered to his hands in his lap. "How else do you get anyone to listen?"

————————

Izzy, Darby, and Jake were the last to leave the school. Shane and Jason had left together. Sarah took her van home.

"Where's your car?" Izzy asked Jake. "Can I have a ride?"

"Sure. I'm in the back parking lot. We'll need to go out this door." He led the way through the hall to the outside.

"I don't come this way very often," Darby commented.

Izzy turned his head to look at the unfamiliar side of the school. "What's that?"

Jake's gaze followed Izzy's pointing finger. Scrawled on the brick walls of the school in black paint were the words, "Killjoy was here." Izzy reached over to touch the paint. "It's dry. Someone must have done this while we were all in the media room."

"I don't get it," Jake said. "What's this supposed to mean?"

"Who's Killjoy?" Darby asked, confused. "I thought the slogan was 'Kil*roy* was here.' "

"Copycat graffiti," Izzy said. "It's a takeoff on the graffiti slogan 'Kilroy was here.' "

"*This* is a take off on the Kilroy of World War II?"

Darby put her hands on her hips and stared at the scrawl. "Who at Brentwood High would do a thing like this?"

The three exchanged glances. The same name was on all their lips, but it was Jake who spoke. "Jason Danier?"

"But he was with us this afternoon," Darby protested. "It couldn't have been him."

That meant there was someone else at Brentwood High who was just as interested in graffiti as Jason and the *Live!* crew. This was an entirely new twist.

"But if it wasn't Jason, who was it?" Izzy pondered.

CHAPTER 6

LIVE FROM DRENTWOOD HIGH

Do not write on the walls.

* * *

We have to. It's too hard to type.

Suddenly, "Killjoy" was everywhere. It was as though he had emerged full blown from the information Izzy had collected on his computer. Everyone in school was talking about it.

"I've had enough of this." Julie threw her chemistry book to the floor and stamped her foot in anger. "Who got into my locker and did this?" She pointed inside the metal door, where "Killjoy was here" was scrawled across the mirror she kept there.

"That's nothing," Molly retorted. "Look at my trigonometry book." She held it out for inspection. "Killjoy was here" was written on nearly every page.

"Did you see it on the sidewalks when you came to school this morning?" Jake asked.

"And over the front door of the school," Josh added, his brown eyes wide with amazement. "Someone used a ladder to get up there."

"I don't understand how this is happening. 'Killjoy' must be pretty athletic."

"And sneaky," Andrew added. "When I walked by the principal's office this morning, he was talking to his secretary. Apparently, Killjoy had gotten into his office and written, 'Killjoy was here' on the blotter on the principal's desk."

"Why now?" Molly wondered aloud.

"Maybe someone heard about the story we're working on," Jake suggested, "and decided to play a joke on the whole school."

"It's a pretty elaborate joke," Izzy commented, "considering all the tactically impossible places this is showing up. Whoever is doing it has done some research. He or she obviously *knows* that the original Kilroy motto turned up in places that seemed nearly impossible to get to."

"Teachers were in the hall discussing it this morning," Josh said. "They didn't know if they should laugh or be angry. Every blackboard in the high school has had 'Killjoy was here' written on it since this whole thing started."

"Everyone is being a copycat artist," Izzy pointed out. "We'll probably never find out who actually started this thing because so many are imitating it."

At that moment, Mr. Clemens, one of the school janitors, came down the hall pushing his rolling scrub bucket. He had a grim expression on his face and a mop slung over one shoulder. It made him look like a bizarre soldier marching off to war. Some of the cleaning rags attached to one side of the bucket fell to the floor.

"I think you dropped something," Jake said.

Mr. Clemens stopped to pick them up. "I don't know what this world is coming to," Mr. Clemens said.

Jake took a step backward.

"I don't mean you, son," Mr. Clemens said, seeing the surprise on Jake's face. "I just got a call from the wood-working shop. Someone has been writing on the walls in there too. The janitorial staff can't keep up with this crazy 'Killjoy' thing. I'm going to have to start working overtime. If I could retire early, I would.

" 'Killjoy was here!' Ha! What *is* this world coming to?" Mr. Clemens turned to walk away, shaking his head. "Graffiti is driving everyone crazy!"

———

Jake, Darby, and Izzy were the only students in the media room when Jason entered. He looked guilty, as if he shouldn't be there.

Izzy stood up and waved him in. "Hi! Come on in and sit down. We're working on your story. Your timing is perfect." Izzy had been ecstatic ever since Jason had relented and agreed to be interviewed.

Jason's eyes darted from side to side and his jaw tightened. The corner of his mouth jumped with a small tic.

"Izzy, I came to talk to you about that story. I don't think I want to do it anymore. I can't help you."

"You can't? Why not?"

"You have to ask after everything that's been going on?" Jason was dumbfounded.

"What are you talking about?"

"All this graffiti stuff." Jason waved an arm toward the hall. "Everyone in the school is talking about it now. Where have you been? In a cave?"

"That doesn't have anything to do with you and the Last Chance Ranch."

"It doesn't?" Jason wore a scornful expression. "Think about it. I got here on Monday, and by Friday someone's scribbling 'Killjoy was here' all over the school. No way am I going to help with a story that will remind anyone that I came from the Last Chance Ranch. Do you know who's going to get blamed for this?" Jason pointed a finger at his own chest. "Me."

At first Darby had thought Jason was angry when he'd entered the media room. Now she saw that his emotion was a combination of nervousness and simple fear. He was new here and, worse yet, a former resident of the Last Chance Ranch. If they hadn't been together when those first words were painted, she too might have suspected him of doing the dirty work.

"Come on, Jason," Izzy pleaded. "We need you for this interview. We'll protect your privacy."

"I think Jason's right," Darby said. "There's no way he can have a fresh start if we keep bringing up his past. The timing isn't good. I don't blame him."

Jason shot her a grateful look.

"It's not as though I don't want to do it," he hesitated, "but I just don't dare."

Izzy was disappointed. "Let's just not say 'never,' " he pleaded. "We'll see how things with 'Killjoy' unfold. Let's put the interview on the back burner for a couple of days."

"Thanks," Jason's shoulders sagged with relief.

"Maybe it seems dumb, but I really do want a fresh start. I've had a pretty lousy life and I'm sick of it. I don't want anything to mess up this chance too."

"Will Jason Danier please come to the office?" The school loudspeaker flickered to life.

Darby was scrolling through words on the teleprompter in the studio. Jake and Izzy tinkered with a broken wheel on one of the cameras while Gary Richmond supervised.

"He's not in here," Gary spoke to the loudspeaker. He looked at Izzy with a raised eyebrow.

"Try study hall," Izzy suggested.

"Thank you." The speaker grew still.

"What do you think they want Jason for?" Izzy asked.

"He's not in any sort of trouble, is he?" Darby asked.

"Now, why would you say that? Just because he came from the Last Chance Ranch?"

Darby blushed. "Maybe. That wasn't very fair, was it?"

"No wonder he's having a hard time getting along here," Izzy muttered. "You're about as fair as people come, Darby, and even *you* can't get it out of your head that he was a troublemaker. Poor guy. He's never going to get a break."

Gary frowned and stood up. "I think I'd better go to the office."

"Why? You said you'd be here all hour."

"That was before I heard this conversation." Gary

tipped his head toward the loudspeaker. "Rumor has it in the teacher's lounge that Mr. Wentworth is planning to interview some of the more suspicious students about where they were when the walls of the school were defaced. He's very unhappy about the graffiti and wants to put an end to it. I have a hunch he'll come down hard on whoever did it."

"And he thinks that might be Jason?" Izzy's expression darkened. "Just because he came here from the ranch?"

"That's my guess. After hearing what you just said, I'd like to have a little talk with Mr. Wentworth before he speaks to Jason."

"Then we should come too." Jake, Darby, and Izzy all stood.

"I can handle this."

"You don't understand! We were *with* Jason when the painting was done. He *couldn't* have done it!"

"Come on, then, before Wentworth gives Jason the third degree."

When they reached the administration offices, Jason was nowhere in sight.

"He's in Mr. Wentworth's office," the secretary said primly. "Mr. Wentworth doesn't want to be disturbed."

"I think perhaps he should be disturbed anyway," Gary said. "He may be making a serious mistake."

"Sir?"

"May I speak to him by phone?"

Gary was hard to turn down when he set his mind to something. He must have been awesome in his photojournalist days, persisting until the story was his.

He still wouldn't take "no" for an answer. Finally the beleaguered secretary put him through to Mr. Wentworth.

Quickly Gary explained that if Jason was being interviewed about the graffiti incident, it was useless, that he had an alibi for that time period. What's more, Gary hinted that cross-examining a guy newly placed from the Last Chance Ranch might actually do more harm in the long run than good, but "proving" to Jason that there was no point in his even trying to make a fresh start.

Finally Gary hung up the phone and turned to the secretary. "He said we should come in."

"All of you?"

"*All* of us." With that, Gary strode toward the door. The others followed in his wake.

Inside the office, both Jason and Mr. Wentworth were looking very grim.

Jason was pale and angry, his fingers gripping the arms of his chair. His eyes had narrowed with challenge. It appeared it would take little to catapult him out of the chair.

Mr. Wentworth didn't look much better. The graffiti incident had caused him a great deal of concern and the interviewing process was not helping matters at all. He, too, was colorless and tense. His fingers tapped nervously on his desk. Relief showed in his expression when Gary and his crew walked through the door.

"Mr. Richmond." Wentworth looked at the students trailing behind. "Isador? Darby? Jake?" He was obviously not expecting them.

"Gary?" Izzy said hesitantly. "We thought Mr. Wentworth *wanted* to see us."

"He will."

"You'll have to explain yourself, Mr. Richmond."

"Are you interrogating Jason about where he was during the graffiti-writing incident?"

"I am. . . ."

"Because someone saw him doing something suspicious or because of his past history?"

Wentworth was taken aback. "No one actually *saw* him. . . ."

"But because he came from the Last Chance Ranch, you assumed . . ." Gary shook his head. "Never mind. We can discuss that later. Right now I'd like you to hear what these students have to say."

Izzy's mouth dropped open, and Darby felt her tongue tangle in her mouth. It was Jake who spoke. "He was with us, sir—in the media room and studio. Jason walked out of the building with Shane. The paint was dry when we touched it. That means it had to have been done when he was with us. Jason *couldn't* have had anything to do with it."

"I see." Mr. Wentworth stared at Jason. "It seems I have an apology to make to you, Mr. Danier. I judged you rashly. Much as I hate to admit it, perhaps I *did* give too much credence to the fact that you came from the state school. I did the very thing I warned my own faculty not to do. I'm sorry."

Jason stared at the older man, dumbfounded.

"Aren't you going to *say* something?" Gary finally asked.

Still, Jason didn't speak. Finally, with a rosy blush

bleeding up his neck, he stammered, "No adult has ever apologized to me before."

"Then maybe you haven't known the right adults," Gary said softly. He put his hand on Jason's shoulder. "Hopefully some of that will change here at Brentwood High."

Gary stayed behind to talk to Mr. Wentworth as the others filed out into the hall. Jason still appeared stunned by what had happened.

"That was weird," Jason finally managed. "Why'd you guys speak up for me, anyway?"

"Because you didn't deserve to be in trouble. You were with us when the first 'Killjoy' graffiti appeared. Gary figured out why Wentworth wanted to see you and wanted to stop it."

"Why are you watching out for me?" Jason asked. "I don't get it."

"We want you to have a fair chance here, that's all. Everybody should have that."

Jason walked off shaking his head, as if their kindness was too much to absorb.

"Have you seen Izzy today?" Molly hissed to Darby as they met in the hallway.

"Not yet. Why? What's he done now?"

"Here he comes. See for yourself."

Izzy sauntered down the hall, swinging his arms and humming. His huge body made smaller students scatter as he passed. He looked very pleased and self-important—and a good deal like a human billboard.

There were buttons tacked all over the front of his

shirt, each proclaiming a different message. *Eat Your Heart Out, I'm Taken. Me, Tense? Of Course Not. My Hair Always Stands On End. I'm Lots Cuter Than I Look.*

"What's this?" Jake walked up to him and tapped him on his *Stop Air Pollution* button.

"Walking graffiti. Isn't it great? I've been reading up on this stuff and it's fascinating. The timing is perfect for our graffiti story. Want to hear what I've learned?"

"Do we have a choice?" Molly muttered.

"Walking graffiti is really no different than the stuff people write on walls," Izzy explained. "In fact, these days it would be hard to tell which came first, the wall or the button. Sort of like the chicken and the egg, get it? Which came first, the chicken or the egg?"

"Get on with it, Izzy. If we have to listen, you have to stay on the subject. And let's keep walking. We're supposed to be in the media room right now."

He sighed, but continued talking as they started out. "Buttons are one way of telling the world what you think, what your opinions are, who you are. It's the same thing a graffiti artist is trying to convey on walls. He's got an opinion he wants to express.

"Political campaign buttons used to be the main use of buttons, but now you see everything from *I'm So Bored, I Might Have To Go To Work* to my dad's favorite, *Older Than Dirt.*"

"But some buttons are just plain dumb," Molly said. "What about those?"

"Most people who wear buttons are willing to talk

about them. They're conversation starters, if nothing else."

"What does this one mean?" Molly pointed to a round blue button that said, *Melville Eats Blubber.* "That's really stupid."

"Melville was the author of the book *Moby Dick*, the story of the whale. Didn't you read it in Literature class?"

"Oh, *that*!" Molly stared at the button for a moment. "It's kind of funny, after all!"

"I love this stuff." Izzy patted the buttons.

"You're *defending* graffiti!" Molly blurted as they entered Chaos Central. Several students looked up to see who Molly was talking to.

"Maybe I am. It's been around since ancient times. Some of what's been found looks like scribbles and scratches, but other bits are very artistic and depict life and animals of the times in which they were drawn. Isn't that a lot like graffiti today?"

"Are you sure it's been around that long?" Andrew asked. He was sitting at a computer, wearing a doubtful expression.

"There's proof of it since A.D. 79."

"Like you have any proof!"

"Actually, I do." Izzy rooted through his backpack and pulled out a book. "Here are pictures taken in Pompeii. When Mount Vesuvius erupted, it covered the entire city with ash and cinders, leaving everything beneath intact. Even the graffiti."

Izzy opened the book to some dark but recognizable photos of walls on which words had been written.

"Some of this is the type of thing you'd find on a

bulletin board at the supermarket—things for sale, lost and found, entertainment notices—and the rest is just stupid stuff."

"Like 'Killjoy was here'?"

"You've got it."

"Things are different now," Andrew said. "I can't imagine my mom or dad writing on walls to communicate!"

Julie and Kate burst out laughing at the image of the refined Mr. and Mrs. Tremaine spray painting walls with messages.

"Probably not," Izzy admitted. "It was a middle- and lower-class 'thing.' Also, lots of children did it."

"How do you know that?" Sarah challenged.

"By the height of the words and pictures from the ground."

Sarah blushed. "I should have thought of that."

"Actually," Izzy mused, "what are school blackboards but walls that we have permission to write on?"

"It's scary, but that makes sense in a twisted way!" Darby said.

"And children in underdeveloped countries learn to read and write on the outdoor walls in their villages. What makes it reading and writing in one country and vandalism in another?" Izzy looked proud of his argument.

"You're talking about scribbling on walls like it's a good idea!" Julie protested. "It's destructive, expensive, and a waste of time."

"It's also art—and a part of our history."

"Just because something has been done for a long

time doesn't mean it's good," Julie pointed out logically. "Maybe it just shows that we're not smart enough to quit doing things when we should!"

The debate grew more and more heated until finally Ms. Wright decided to step in.

"No matter what might be good about graffiti, Isador, the fact is that it's a destructive and expensive means of expression. Brentwood's city officials are very upset about the 'artwork' decorating the buildings around town. Old art form or new, we don't have the right to deface or destroy the property of others. Would you agree with that?"

Shane, who'd been quiet until now, spoke up. "I would."

"I thought you were on my side," Izzy growled.

"I didn't know we were taking sides. I agree with Ms. Wright. I like street art, but it shouldn't ruin property."

"Then what's the solution?" Darby asked.

Ms. Wright snapped her fingers. "That's what the four of you are going to find out. I can hardly wait to see your story!"

Izzy, Darby, Jake, and Shane groaned in unison. They'd been had. Ms. Wright had brought them around to the whole purpose of their assignment.

"You're good, Ms. Wright," Izzy said grudgingly as he pulled out a notebook and set to work. "Really good."

CHAPTER 7

LIVE FROM BRENTWOOD HIGH

UFOs are real;

the airforce doesn't exist.

After the incident in Mr. Wentworth's office, Izzy's relationship with Jason changed. Jason finally warmed to Izzy's offered friendship. Whatever hostility and mistrust Jason had harbored for Jake, Darby, and Gary had also evaporated with their show of support. Though he remained aloof from most of the other students except Shane, whom he'd immediately hit it off with, he allowed Izzy inside the wall he'd built around himself.

"Want to study with us tonight?" Izzy asked Jason as they were leaving the school. Shane, Darby, and Jake were loaded down with stacks of textbooks. "Midterm tests tomorrow."

"You guys actually *study*?" Jason scoffed.

Izzy's eyes narrowed. "Actually, we do."

"Why?"

Darby held her breath. Jason was in one of his rebellious moods. She'd seen it in class. So far he'd avoided a confrontation, but one day he was going to take things too far and end up in trouble. Izzy and Shane seemed to be the only two people who could talk him out of this attitude when it appeared.

"So we can stay in school, graduate, and go on to college," Izzy said sharply. "And not mess up our lives and end up in reform school."

Darby groaned inwardly. Why did Izzy have to say that? Jason looked positively furious now.

Then a slight smile tipped one corner of his mouth. "Really? Is that what I did wrong?"

Jake and Darby stared at the pair in dumbfounded amazement. "What just happened here?" Jake finally asked.

Jason turned to Jake. "Izzy plays it straight with me. I like that."

"I thought you were going to pound him."

"I considered it." Jason eyed the stack of books in Darby's arms. "Do you want me to help you carry those? If we're going to study together, I'd better help out."

The dangerous moment passed. They left the school together. Izzy and Jason drove together in Izzy's car while Shane and Darby went with Jake.

As they drove toward the Mooney's house, Darby asked Shane, "Why didn't Jason just hit Izzy in the teeth back there?"

"Because he likes Izzy. And because he knows Izzy is right."

"Jason has a bad temper," she observed.

"If he didn't, he probably wouldn't have ended up at the Last Chance Ranch in the first place. I've heard that he is quite a fighter," Jake pointed out.

Of all those in media class, Shane understood Jason best. "Izzy dared to say what no one else would. I respect that. Jason did too."

"I don't understand," Darby said.

"Have you noticed how people tiptoe around Jason? I know he doesn't give off very friendly vibes, but everybody treats him like a time bomb ready to explode. That gets old. Izzy treats him like a person. Wouldn't you prefer that to having people walk around you never saying what they really think?"

"Sure, when you put it that way." Darby studied the backs of her hands for a few moments before venturing another question. "You are a lot like Jason, aren't you, Shane?"

Shane was quiet for a long time. Darby began to worry that she'd asked too personal a question.

"Yes. I am." He stared out the window of the car. Jake and Darby remained silent, almost breathless. "I'd probably be in Jason's position if it weren't for a few lucky breaks."

When he looked at them, his eyes were cloudy. "I've had a few brushes with the law. Jason's life could have been mine. It's mind-boggling to think about it. Jason's presence here has opened my eyes."

"Are you different now?" Darby took it a step further.

Shane gave a humorless laugh. "Am I? I don't know. I'm trying."

"We can see that. You're much more friendly than you used to be."

"Mr. Personality, that's me." Once again Shane

stared through the car window, intent on something neither Jake nor Darby could see. "Actually, I never saw any reason to *be* different until I stared to work on the *Live! From Brentwood High* program.

"Ms. Wright is cool. She doesn't hound me like other teachers do. She makes me *want* to work for her. And Gary is so . . . knowing. It's like he's lived my life and a dozen others as well. I've never known adults like them before."

A faint spill of pink crawled up Shane's neck to his cheeks. "And the students aren't bad either."

"Is that a compliment?" Jake demanded. "If it is, I want to know about it."

"See? That's what I mean," Shane continued. "Nobody acts scared of me, either. I like that. I guess you guys have just begun to feel like . . . friends."

"We *are* friends!" Darby said adamantly. "Haven't you figured that out yet?"

Shane sighed. "I haven't had many, except the kind in gangs, and they aren't always very reliable."

"You and Jason *are* two of a kind! Suspicious, mistrusting, antisocial. . . ." Impulsively, Darby threw her arms around Shane's neck.

"That's the first time anyone has said that about me and made it sound like a compliment," he said with an embarrassed laugh.

"Don't worry. We won't give up on either of you," Darby assured him.

Then she glanced at the street sign they'd just passed. "Two blocks to Izzy's place. Do you want to hand me some of those books?"

Izzy's little sister Heidi opened the door. She was wearing a pink-and-white jogging suit and tiny name-brand sneakers. "My brother's in the refrigerator. Do you want to come in?"

"I knew Izzy spent a lot of time in the refrigerator," Jake commented, "but I didn't realize he'd moved in permanently."

Heidi chortled at the remark. "No, silly! He's getting something to eat." Then she stuck her finger in her mouth. "And me and my sister are supposed to 'disappear' when you come. Gotta go. Bye." With that, she vanished up the stairs.

"That was quick," Darby commented. "Usually the girls hang around and ask questions."

"I bribed them." Izzy entered the foyer carrying a twelve-pack of soda. "Three games of 'Uncle Wiggley' and a candy bar if they'd leave us alone. The twins would drive us nuts if we let them stay."

They followed Izzy into the living room and settled their books on the coffee table. When food, sodas, and texts had been sorted through and put in the proper places, Izzy leaned back in his recliner and sighed. "I hate tests."

"You? Why? You always ace them."

"Correction. You always *expect* me to ace them. The pressure is murder."

Jason made a sound of disbelief. "I've never 'aced' a test in my life. The only thing that I'm even a little good at is art, and who cares about that?"

Jake snapped his fingers. "That reminds me. I

heard something about you today."

Jason stiffened and his eyes darkened.

"Don't worry. It's not bad. I heard the art teacher say she had a new student in her class who showed 'great promise' and that she hoped he'd enter the student art show next month."

"Oh, that." Jason looked embarrassed. "I just drew her a picture of some squirrels, that's all."

"I heard her talking about it in the hallway," Jake continued. "She said those animals looked alive on the paper and that you had exceptional talent."

"When did you start eavesdropping, Jake?" Shane inquired with a sneer.

"When I hear good things about my friends," Jake shot back. "Am I ever going to hear something good about you?"

"Break it up," Izzy ordered cheerfully. Then he clapped Jason on the back. "Good going. Exceptional, huh?"

Jason was thoughtful. Softly, so that his words were nearly imperceptible, he murmured, *"Exceptional."*

It was obviously the first time Jason had ever felt exceptional about anything.

A bird in the hand

can be messy.

"I've got it!" Izzy crashed into the media room as class was about to begin. His broad face was pink with enthusiasm and exertion. His jean jacket hung off one shoulder and both shoes were untied.

"If you've 'got it,' you'd better either plan to share it with the rest of the class or take 'it' home to bed until you're over it," Ms. Wright said dryly.

She pushed her reading glasses from the tip of her nose to its bridge, but they slid down again. She was wearing a huge soft sweater over a gauzy ankle-length skirt and lace-up western-style boots. Her hair was gathered into a tousled knot atop her head. Her earrings hung to her shoulders, and a pendant depicting a yawning cat decorated her outfit. Only Ms. Wright could look good—no, stunning—in such a costume.

Her dry comment brought Izzy to a halt.

He looked around the room as if he were realizing

for the first time where he was. His gaze fell on Shane. "There you are. We've got to talk."

"Isador..." Rosie Wright cleared her throat in a soft warning.

"It's about our story," Izzy explained. "I've got the perfect way to research our piece on the Last Chance Ranch."

"Then we might as well start with that," Ms. Wright assessed. "Gary, do you mind?"

Gary was slouched in the corner, watching what was transpiring. "Not at all."

"I've asked Gary to discuss filming at night, in daylight, with fluorescents, and with baselights," Ms. Wright explained. "Some of the lighting with our interviews out of the studio hasn't been what it should be. But if he doesn't mind, Isador, you may tell us all what's so wonderful about your idea first."

Izzy marched to the podium. He winked at Sarah and then fixed his gaze on Shane. "Last night I couldn't get to sleep. I had this feeling that our story on the Last Chance Ranch was too important to give just a glossy overview. But how do we get a really in-depth story? Something that hasn't already been done? A view of the *people* at the ranch and not just the facility?"

Darby and Jake both looked up, aware that Izzy had been thinking about Jason.

"Finally, it came to me! The only way for us to do a good job is for Shane and I to spend a couple of days at the ranch as 'inmates' and see exactly what it's like."

"What?" Shane nearly toppled his desk when he

shot up. "Are you *crazy*? Get ourselves locked up in that place? No way. I'm staying out of there, thank you."

"But it's the perfect way to get the story!"

"Listen, Izzy, you're going too far with this one. I've known a lot of people who've spent time at the ranch, and none of them ever want to go back. Why should I intentionally put myself through that?" Shane's voice shook.

"If we do this story, maybe a few others will get the same idea. If just one person straightens out because of us ..."

"Quit dreaming," Shane retorted sharply. "Staying *out* of that place is my best motivation for staying on the right side of the law. I'm not going to mess with that."

"Exactly!" Izzy crowed. "Let's tell everyone why they should keep clean and not mess with trouble. I think seeing the ranch from the inside for a couple days would do that." He turned to the rest of the class. "What do the rest of you think?"

Josh shrugged. "I wouldn't want to do it, but it's up to you."

"Overnight? In a place like that?" Andrew shuddered. "No thanks."

"How do you know what 'a place like that' is?" Sarah questioned. "So far we're all just guessing. Maybe if you've been in trouble it's a good place to be. Better than prison, I'll bet."

"I think Izzy and Shane *should* be locked up. And they should throw away the key," Julie said. "Who deserves it more?"

Ms. Wright stepped in just as Izzy was about to respond. "Enough. Julie, Izzy, no bickering."

"But she—"

"I know." Ms. Wright smiled at Izzy. "But I want to tell you what *I* think of your idea—just in case you're interested."

Izzy blushed. "I'd planned to talk to you and Shane about it first, but when you said to tell the whole class . . ."

"It's fine, Isador. Actually, it's more than fine. I think it's an excellent idea."

"You do?" the class gasped in unison.

"I've been teaching a class out there," she continued calmly, "and I've found it very educational for myself as well. It's a good facility. Well run. There is a lot of compassion for the boys who live there. Granted, I'm only there a few hours a week, but I've been impressed with what I've seen. I believe I could arrange it so you boys could go in to the facility one day and leave the next. '24 Hours At the Last Chance Ranch.' An interesting title, don't you think?"

"You mean we could actually *do* it?" The wind was knocked from Izzy's sails when his glorious idea became nitty-gritty reality.

"Why not? Boys are processed in and out quite regularly. You'd have to wear the Last Chance uniforms, of course, and cut your hair. . . ."

"Not me!" Shane glared at Izzy. "And I think it's a really stupid idea."

Izzy ran his fingers over his buzz cut. "I suppose a haircut wouldn't hurt me." He paused. "But we'd be staying overnight?"

"Are you getting scared?" Andrew asked. He made little clucking sounds with his tongue. "Chicken!"

Izzy took a step toward him, but Ms. Wright put her hand on Izzy's arm. "Don't let him get to you," she advised. "There may be guys at the ranch who will taunt you in the same way. It will be up to you to handle it properly."

"Mooney, you've lost your mind," Shane growled, obviously upset about the idea of spending time at the ranch.

"Don't go, then," Kate said. "Stay home."

Andrew renewed the clucking sounds.

"It would make a great story," Darby pointed out, "but it wouldn't be very good television. There wouldn't be anything to see except us interviewing Izzy and Shane when they returned."

"Not if I went with them." Gary's voice from the back of the room startled them all.

"You? How?"

"We could do a documentary. I'd follow the guys through every stage of their first day at the ranch. News shows do it all the time. If Rosie can clear it with the ranch's officials, I'll do it."

"You'd stay all night?" Izzy asked, a hint of relief in his voice.

"If they'd let me. I'd keep the camera rolling as much as possible, and we'd edit later."

"Shouldn't we be the ones doing the camera work?" Josh inquired. "After all, it's our project."

"It's unlikely that they would let amateurs do such a thing in that setting. Besides, I've spent a lot of years at this. I can make myself pretty invisible behind a camera if I want."

"Gary is right. He'd be best. It would also give Izzy and Shane someone for moral support," Ms. Wright said.

"I'm not going," Shane muttered.

"As you wish. Jake, would you like to go in Shane's place? You're on this story team, too."

"Wait a minute," Shane held up a hand. "Who says he can go?"

"If you don't, someone else should."

Shane sat back in his chair and crossed his arms over his chest. "Let me think about it. It's just that..."

"It feels funny to consider going into a place you've been afraid of?" Sarah finished.

Shane lowered his eyes.

"I hated going to the hospital, even to visit someone, for a long time after my accident. It represented everything bad and scary to me. Still, when I finally broke down and went to see our neighbor and her new baby, it wasn't so bad. It was just a place, a building." Sarah looked at Shane. "If you go, they aren't going to *keep* you, you know. You haven't done anything *wrong*, have you?"

Shane smiled. "No, not lately."

"And if fear of the Last Chance Ranch has kept you from that, it's probably a pretty *good* place, right?"

"Only you, Sarah," he groaned. "You could talk an Eskimo into buying a bikini."

"Then, you'll do it?" Ms. Wright asked with a smile.

"I guess." Shane didn't look happy.

"Then we'd better get busy. I teach there the day after tomorrow."

––––––––

The door swung shut behind Shane and Izzy, snapping closed with a sound of permanence neither could ignore. Shane glared at Izzy. "This was your bright idea, Knucklehead. Now what?"

"The counselor said he'd be right back with clothes." Izzy squirmed restlessly. "I feel like I've got bugs crawling all over me."

"Nerves," Shane said unsympathetically. "And you deserve it. How'd I let you talk me into this anyway? It's creepy."

"It's not so bad." Izzy looked around the room. "It's clean. The floor looks like you could eat off it."

"Let's hope we don't have to."

"Come on, Shane, ease up. We're just staying at the Last Chance Ranch overnight. Gary's going to be around with the camera. All we have to do is see how it feels."

"It feels lousy." Shane would not relent.

"You came really close to ending up in here, didn't you?" Izzy asked softly.

Shane stared at him. "How do you know that?"

"By the way you're acting. I've never seen you scared before."

"I'm not scared now."

"No? Then relax and quit hanging onto the back of

that chair like it's a life preserver. This isn't permanent."

At that moment, Mr. Wang entered. He was a pleasant-looking man in his mid-forties with a brisk, no-nonsense manner. He handed each of them a set of clothing and a pile of bedding and towels.

"We've already had the first head count for the night. Last count and lights out is at ten-thirty. Your cameraman will bunk in one of the guest rooms and you two will be together in this double room. That way you can get up for the six-thirty head count and start the day like the other boys."

"Will they think this is weird?" Izzy asked, his wonderful idea seeming considerably less wonderful in the harsh light of reality.

"They've been told what's going on. You can't tape any of the boys without permission, but the ones who've agreed to talk to you will be around. The others will stay off camera." Mr. Wang paused to study the pair. "It's very impressive that you boys are willing to do this for your class."

"We've done a lot of crazy things for the *Live! From Brentwood High* show," Izzy admitted. "But we've really learned a lot in the process."

"Keep it up. It says in Proverbs 12:24 that 'diligent hands will rule, but laziness ends in slave labor.' I've seen a lot of good boys gone bad come through here. I like to see kids who have interests and goals. Having time to waste usually means trouble for a teenager."

"Do you think it helps to be in here?" Shane asked. "Other than being off the street, I mean."

"The counseling alone is worth a great deal." Mr.

Wang took off his glasses to rub his eye.

"I lead two Bible study classes," he continued. "They aren't the most popular ones to join, but everyone is required to fill those hours, so many of the boys eventually end up with me."

"Why isn't it popular?" Izzy asked hesitantly.

"Do you belong to a Bible study group at your high school?" Mr. Wang asked.

"No, but . . ."

"Would you consider it?"

"He's got a girlfriend who's a Christian," Shane said, seeing that Izzy was getting flustered.

"Then you *are* open to the idea. Most of the boys who come here are downright hostile to anything that sounds like 'church' or 'religion.' "

"So how do the Bible studies go?" Shane inquired.

"Surprisingly well. Of course, I have a secret technique that I don't tell the boys about."

"What's that?"

Mr. Wang chuckled. "I turn the whole thing over to God. I figure if He can't manage these boys, who can? I've found Him to be a great teaching partner."

Then Mr. Wang became brisk and businesslike again. "You boys had better get some sleep. Tomorrow will be a long day."

———

And tonight will be a long night. The thought rolled through Izzy's mind over and over as he lay in the narrow bunk in the small cubicle he and Shane shared. Above him, he could hear Shane tossing and turning as well.

What would happen tomorrow? What if this actually were to be their home for the next year? Izzy pulled the blanket over his head, hoping to block out the thought.

CHAPTER 9

LIVE

FROM BRENTWOOD HIGH

Don't eat yellow snow.

At six-thirty a sharp bell rang. Izzy woke with a start. He sat up and hit his head on the upper bunk. "Owww!"

"You can say that again! I just fell asleep." Shane's feet appeared over the side of the bed and dangled in Izzy's face.

"You too?" Izzy gingerly touched his forehead. There would probably be a lump, but there was no bleeding. "I must have tossed and turned until four A.M."

Shane slid off the upper bunk and landed in front of Izzy. The guys studied each other critically. In unison, they said, "You look terrible!"

Shane ran his fingers through his hair. "I'd better get an A-plus for this. And a college scholarship. And . . ."

"I know. I'm regretting it too, but look at it this way, we're going to have a great story."

Shane looked around the tiny room. "Now what?"

"Mr. Wang said we should use the shower next

door, dress, and be standing outside our room in"—Izzy looked at his watch—"fifteen minutes!"

The boys whirled into action and were waiting nervously by their door when others started to emerge from their rooms. They were looked over with open curiosity by every young man who entered the hallway. Neither Shane nor Izzy noticed that Gary had followed them until they reached the dining hall.

They watched him maneuver through the dining room. Though some boys noticed Gary, others seemed oblivious to his presence. Shane poked Izzy in the side. "He really can disappear behind that thing, can't he?"

Mr. Wang was there, as crisp and professional as he had been the night before. He made several announcements concerning classes and work schedules before introducing Izzy, Shane, and Gary.

The residents had been forewarned about their presence and interest in them was slight. In fact, they were left standing when the others filed out of the room after breakfast.

Then a thin, wiry boy with a bad complexion broke away from the others and walked toward them. "We make our beds and clean our rooms now. We have class at eight A.M."

―――――

By noon, Izzy and Shane had been through a remedial reading class, math, history, and wood shop. Discipline was tight and there was no opportunity to talk to any of the other residents. Lunch was their first chance to mix.

After the head count, which occurred several times a day, the residents seemed to relax. The same thin boy who'd talked to them earlier brought his tray to the table where Izzy and Shane sat.

"So, how'd it go this morning?" He broke open a carton of milk and chugged it down.

Quietly Gary, who'd been about to leave the room, turned his camera toward the boys.

"Okay. Not much different than our school," Izzy said. "I don't know what I expected, but not that."

"By the way, my name is Norm." He extended a hand. "Mr. Wang told us that we could choose whether or not we wanted to talk to you. I got 'elected.' "

"Why?" Shane asked bluntly. "What's your story?"

"I'm one of Last Chance's big 'successes,' " Norm said with a grin that told them he didn't take the label too seriously. "If you can be a success in a place like this, I am one."

"What does that mean?"

"I was a first-time offender who got messed up with some bad dudes. They robbed a convenience store and shot the guy at the till. I had no idea what they were planning, but I was there when it happened. Fortunately the guy lived, but"—and he shrugged with studied carelessness—"here I am."

"That makes you a success?"

"Nah. It took me a while to get used to life here. I'd been running pretty wild. My parents didn't know what to do with me. In a way, they were relieved that I ended up here. They made me get into counseling and back to school, two things my parents wanted for me but couldn't seem to manage. I'll graduate about the same time I get out."

"Then what?"

"More school, I guess. The crazy thing is, I discovered in here that I'm pretty smart with computers. I've even started to teach a class for the younger kids. Wild, huh?"

"So, have you *learned* anything?" Shane studied Norm over the top of a carton of milk he held to his lips. "Or are you going to make the same mistakes again?"

"No way. This was enough of a wake-up call for me. I'm working on it with my counselor. He's helping me to teach myself to think before I act. Even about little stuff. Now I don't open my mouth or make a move until I think about it first. I get in a lot less trouble that way."

Norm glanced at his watch. "What's your afternoon schedule?"

Izzy pulled the slip of paper Mr. Wang had given him out of his pocket. "Grounds maintenance. Trimming and raking. South of the dormitory."

"At least you get to be outside. I'm stuck in group counseling. I'd better get going. I don't want any demerits now."

After Norm had left for class, Izzy and Shane made their way outside. Their afternoon job involved trimming and raking around the many buildings at the ranch. During the summer, vegetable gardens provided much of the fresh produce used in the kitchen. Now, with the gardens cleaned out and mulched, there was still much outside work to do.

Some residents had drawn work duty in the barns and were busy cleaning stalls and hauling bedding straw to the animals. Others were grinding feed, painting outbuildings, or doing maintenance on the ranch vehicles.

"Are you the guys with the TV show?" A scrawny boy with a cowlick and a swagger moved to where Jake and Izzy were working. The name embroidered on the pocket of his shirt said *Casey*.

"Yeah." Shane glanced around. Gary was casually propped against the wall of a nearby shed, tinkering with his camera.

"You gonna tell the truth about this place?"

" 'Truth'?" Shane repeated cautiously. "Why don't you tell us what the truth is?"

"I hate it here. It stinks. I tried to escape but they caught me." His face contorted with anger. "I thought I had everything planned too. We had a buddy distract the counselors while we got away, but they picked us up hitchhiking. Man, if I coulda gotten away, my life would be a whole lot better."

"Where would you go?" Shane asked mildly. Casey was eager to talk, and Shane was equally eager to listen.

"Find my dad, maybe. My mom's remarried and my stepdad is a jerk. I wouldn't go back there." He shrugged his thin shoulders, trying to look tough. He only succeeded in looking pitiful. "I got buddies— gang members. I'd probably join them. That's what I would have done if I hadn't ended up here."

"A wannabe, huh?" Shane said.

Casey's fingers curled into fists. "Yeah. You got

problems with that?" Casey wanted to prove he was a man. Unfortunately the only way he knew how was by bragging and fighting.

"Not really. I thought about being in a gang once," Shane said.

Izzy looked at him sharply but didn't speak.

"I just decided that I'd rather be my own man, make my own decisions, that's all."

Casey's expression darkened. "I can do that."

"Then, you don't need a gang."

Casey considered Shane's statement. "Then, who's going to stand up for me if I need help?" Many times a gang was the only "family" a guy really had.

"Friends," Izzy suggested. "Your folks."

Casey looked at them scornfully. "You guys don't get it, do you? I don't have those things." He turned away, leaving Izzy and Shane staring at each other.

Before they could speak, a siren began to wail. Its whoop-whoop-whooping sound assaulted their ears, and boys started to run for the main building from all parts of the ranch grounds.

Shane caught Casey by the shoulder before he could disappear too. "What's going on?"

"Runaways. They sound that siren when somebody's missing. I gotta get to the main hall to report in. I don't want them thinking *I* had anything to do with it." He squirmed away from Shane and took off at a dead run.

"Looks like we have some excitement for our program," Gary commented calmly as he walked by the boys. "I'd better keep the tape rolling."

When they arrived, the main hall was filled with excited young men and red-faced counselors attempting damage control.

"What happened?" Izzy negotiated himself into a position next to Norm.

"Two new guys ran away. Instead of going to their afternoon assignments, they must have snuck off after lunch. Some probation counselors went after them, but one of them just came back alone," Norm informed them.

"Now what happens?"

"Security gets boosted for the rest of us," Norm said with a resigned sigh. "Just in case someone else gets the bright idea to try to escape."

"What about the guys who left?"

"Oh, they'll find them. They always do. The county sheriff or highway patrol are probably picking them up right now if they tried to hitch a ride. Everybody knows the Last Chance uniforms. Even if they hide out, they'll have to come out sometime. The longest anyone has ever been away is twenty-four hours, and that's 'cause he lay in a ditch overnight." Norm whistled. "You should have seen the mosquito bites on that guy!"

"Do they punish them when they find them?"

"You bet. Every time you run away, you have to start your time over. I'd be crazy to try to run now because I'm going to be out soon. Some guys do it, though. Usually it's the ones who haven't gotten their heads together. Some of them even risk going to prison."

Izzy and Shane both felt a cloud of depression descending over them as the day progressed. By recreation time, though, it was as though the two boys' escape attempt had never happened. The structured life of the ranch had returned. The buzz at supper was that the pair had been picked up less than five miles from the school, scared and lost. They were city boys, not familiar with the country.

Head count at supper was thorough and deliberate, a telling reminder that inmates of Last Chance Ranch were closely observed.

Because Shane and Izzy did not have an evening counseling assignment, they were allowed free time in the recreation room. They walked together down the hall toward the large multipurpose room.

"This is getting to me," Shane muttered. "I feel like things are closing in."

"But this is the first time we've been free to do what we want!"

"Free? We're 'free' to be where they want us to be, to do what they want us to do. We can watch a silly kids' movie with no violence, play Ping-Pong, lift weights, or read books they've picked out for us. What would you be doing if you were home right now?" Shane asked.

Izzy grew thoughtful. "Calling Sarah, probably. We'd do our homework together over the phone. Or playing a game with the twins. Maybe I'd help Grandma with dishes or shoot hoops with Jake or Josh. . . . That sure seems like a long time ago, in another world. I miss my life!"

"And we've only been here about twenty hours,"

Shane pointed out. "What if we knew this was going to *be* our lives for the next few months?"

They were still considering the idea when Mr. Wang approached them. "Boys, I'd like to talk to you."

Warily, they followed the counselor to some chairs in a corner of the room.

"I have someone who is willing to give you an interview," Wang began. "Frankly, I'm surprised that he will talk, but he says he will. He seems genuinely interested in helping you—and warning others not to follow in his footsteps. Your cameraman is setting up in my office. He said I should come to get you."

The expression on Mr. Wang's face was puzzling, a mixture of surprise and apprehension.

"What's this guy's story?" Shane asked. "Why is he here?"

"Maybe he should tell you."

"I think it would help to have some warning."

Mr. Wang studied the boys for a moment. "Murder. He's here because he murdered someone."

Zane Cunningham didn't look like a murderer. He looked more like a paper boy or a gas jockey or a stock boy at the grocery store.

He was blond and tanned like an outdoor athlete. His cheeks still held a hint of baby fat, and it was obvious that he didn't need to shave every day. He wore his uniform with a flair, his shoulders flung back and his collar at an angle, which made it look slightly different than all the other identical uniforms at the ranch.

When Izzy and Shane entered the office, Gary was explaining to Zane about the *Live! From Brentwood High* program and the current documentary they were producing. Zane was engrossed with Gary's equipment and had to work hard to pull himself away from the elaborate camera.

Mr. Wang introduced the boys and quickly disappeared, leaving Izzy and Shane to stare in curiosity and fascination at the young man in front of them.

Izzy, never one to hold back his thoughts, blurted, "You don't look like you killed someone!"

Gary shook his head behind the camera, and Shane jabbed Izzy in the ribs with his elbow. Only Zane didn't seem to mind Izzy's bluntness.

"No? Guess all murderers don't look like you'd expect."

Shane took over. He pulled three chairs in line with the filming equipment and indicated that Zane should sit in one of them. He pushed Izzy into another. The light on the camera told him that it was already rolling.

"Why did you agree to talk to us?" Shane asked.

"Something to do. I get stuck in every single counseling session this place has. This can't be any more boring than that."

"Mr. Wang told us he thought you wanted to warn people not to do what you did."

"Do you want me to start at the beginning?" Zane seemed more in control of the interview than the others.

According to his story, Zane had been a drug dealer by the age of fifteen. He'd sold crack cocaine and owned a gun and a motorcycle.

He'd been in a bad mood the night of the murder. His girlfriend had broken up with him. For that reason, when another guy, whom Zane suspected of trying to "horn in" on his territory, had confronted Zane about a drug deal, Zane had pulled out his gun and shot him. Just like that. With no forethought. Dead.

It was chilling to hear this handsome young man talk so matter-of-factly about what he had done. Izzy shivered. Shane didn't move in his chair.

"Maybe you guys saw some of the publicity after the murder," Zane said. "Because of my age, it was a big deal. I was on TV a lot but they always blocked out my face."

"*You're* the one?" Izzy gasped. "I remember now. The press went crazy!"

"Tell me about it. My parents had to move out of their house 'cause nobody would leave them alone." He laughed without humor. "No, that's not quite true. It was reporters who wouldn't leave them alone. The neighbors quit talking to them. I guess they wanted my folks out. They were afraid when I got released I'd come home, and they didn't want me around the neighborhood."

Zane's frankness was shocking. Shane decided to take advantage of it.

"Had you used your gun before?"

"A couple times, to scare people away. I'd never actually hit anybody before." He grew pensive. "I didn't mean to hit anyone then, either. I was just going to scare him, that's all. The jerk had been messing around in my territory. I was afraid he was gonna take away some of my business. I thought if I waved the gun around, he'd know I meant business and leave me alone."

Izzy and Shane were as silent as two deer frozen in oncoming headlights, neither wanting to interrupt Zane's story. The camera was focused on Zane's face.

"It was weird. I'd handled the gun before, but somehow it felt heavier that day. It was pulling my hand down like a weight. I'd been knocking around a handball the day before. Maybe my wrist was weak. Who knows? Anyway, when I pulled the trigger, I meant to aim over his head." His blue eyes darkened to black marbles. "Instead I shot him in the face."

There was absolute silence in the room. Even Gary seemed to be holding his breath. Finally, Zane spoke. "I've thought about it a lot since then," he said softly. "I wish I'd never had that gun. If it weren't for that, I might have punched the guy in the stomach or something, but I wouldn't have *killed* him.

"I go to anger counseling now. I'm supposed to be learning to control my anger, but it isn't easy. Not much helps."

Zane began to blush, something he hadn't done even while talking graphically about the murder. "Do you want to know what helps me with my anger?" he asked. "It's something I learned here."

"Sure," Izzy breathed. "What is it?"

"Two verses I repeat to myself. 'Do not be quickly provoked in your spirit, for anger resides in the lap of fools' (Ecclesiastes 7:9). And 'A quick-tempered man does foolish things. . . . ' (Proverbs 14:17)."

Zane blushed. "Can you believe it? I can't. *Me*, spouting *Bible verses*!" Then a slow grin split his features. "But it works. That's why I agreed to talk to you on television. God's changed my life. Sometimes, when it's really quiet and I think about what I did, I get cold all over. *I killed a man.* But God loves me enough to forgive me for that. That's a lot of love. Nobody else has ever loved me that much. Not my family. Not my friends. So I just wanted to tell somebody else about it. I figured you guys could . . . you know . . . get the word out."

Izzy's face was a radiant mixture of surprise, pleasure, and affection. "My girlfriend's a Christian. She's going to be really happy with what you just said."

"Good. Then at least one person will understand. A lot of the guys in here don't. They think I'm crazy." Zane smiled sadly. "They're like I *used* to be."

"How's that?"

"When it first happened, I didn't feel much of anything—no regret, no sorrow—because the guy I killed was scum like me, maybe worse because he tried to peddle drugs to really little kids. I almost felt like I'd done the world a favor.

"It wasn't until I learned about Jesus that I began to feel bad. Then I realized that Jesus loved that guy too—that He could have changed his life in the same way He's changed mine."

For the first time, Zane's eyes clouded with tears. "I took a life away that could have been changed. Now it's too late, and I'll never forget how wrong that was."

Zane tried to look tough for the silent eye of the camera, but the tears coursing down his cheeks told the truth. Gently Shane reached out and put his arm across Zane's trembling shoulders. Just as quietly, Izzy laid a hand on the guy's knee. None of them noticed when Gary turned off the camera and left the room.

CHAPTER 10

LIVE

FROM BRENTWOOD HIGH

Have you hugged a student today?

Izzy and Shane were silent as they drove away from the Last Chance Ranch in Gary's ten-year-old car. It wasn't until they stopped for burgers at a fast food place on the outskirts of Brentwood that either of them spoke. Then the floodgates opened and words came pouring out.

"Even the *air* smells better here! And these burgers ... great, aren't they?"

"If I'd had to go through head count one more time, I think I'd have gone crazy."

"Can you imagine being there for *months*?"

"Or *years*?" Shane asked.

Neither of them had been able to quit thinking about Zane and the story he'd told.

"Better than prison, I guess," Izzy said. "Maybe Zane's lucky. I'd rather be at the ranch. Because he's a juvenile his sentence is shorter, too."

"I interviewed Mr. Wang while you were packing," Shane said. "He told me that almost half the kids are arrested again within a few months."

"That many? Why?"

"According to him, it's pretty easy to behave inside the ranch. There's both discipline and caring there, things usually missing at home for these guys. When they go back, they revert to their old ways."

"Don't Mr. Wang and the other counselors get discouraged?"

"He said the burn-out rate is high, but they're all committed to making a difference for kids." Shane stared out the window. "I never realized how many people there were who actually *cared*."

The *Live! From Brentwood High* staff viewed all the tapes Gary had made at the ranch. No one said a word until the last tape was done.

Then Sarah spoke. "That was the most amazing thing I've ever seen!"

"How'd you guys *stand* it?" Andrew squirmed in his chair. "I would have lost my mind!"

"Tell us about every minute from the time you got there until the time you left," Molly demanded. "I want to hear everything."

Willingly, Izzy and Shane obliged. Their need to talk about what they'd experienced was as great as the rest of the crew's need to hear it. The previous thirty-six hours had affected them deeply. Even Shane was eager to express what those hours had meant to him.

The Last Chance Ranch might have been the primary topic of conversation for weeks if "Killjoy" hadn't diverted the entire school's attention.

A graffiti epidemic had broken out in Brentwood. So many buildings were newly pockmarked with spray-painted drawings and symbols that no one could ignore the problem. Even some of the school buses had been targeted, along with every outside wall of the school and gymnasium. The situation left the faculty and the student body frustrated and curious.

"Who's *doing* this?" Kate demanded. "That's what I want to know."

"You and everybody else," Andrew sneered. "If they knew who was doing it, they could arrest him and put a stop to it."

"I'm not sure it's that easy," Darby countered. "There have to be several people or groups of people doing this, not just one person. There's 'copycat graffiti' going on. Someone started it, and now it's taken off."

"Darby's right. Who knows? Maybe kids are doing it on a dare now. It could be anybody."

"Not all of it," Shane said.

Everyone stared at him. "What do you mean?"

"Not just anyone could do all the graffiti that's up. Have you seen the south side of the school?"

"Oh, yeah. That's almost . . ." Julie searched for a word, ". . . beautiful!"

"Exactly. No scribbler or tagger did that. Whoever drew on that wall was a real artist."

"That makes it even harder to figure out who's doing it," Darby said. "Too bad. It would be great to report on catching the culprit on the *Live!* report."

Jake snapped his fingers and jumped to his feet. "Great idea! We can solve the graffiti artist mystery right along with Izzy and Shane's report on the subject!"

"Oh yeah, right," Julie said. "Easy as pie. Figure out who did it. The *police* can't even do that!"

"But I'll bet we could," Jake said. "All we'd have to do is a little brainstorming."

"And you'll have to brainstorm somewhere else." Ms. Wright closed her grade book and stood up. "I have a faculty meeting, and you all need to be out of here tonight. The janitor is waiting to wash and wax the floor."

"But we need to talk!" Jake protested. The others nodded.

"You could come to my place."

Everyone swiveled around to the one who had spoken. Shane sat there calmly, behaving as if he asked friends over after school every day of the year.

No one had ever been to Shane's. No one, that is, that they knew about.

"Your house? Really?"

"Sure. It's okay." He looked at Sarah. "My mom's home today so your parents won't have to . . . worry . . . or anything."

It was the first offer of friendship Shane had made to any of them. No one was willing to refuse.

————

They all piled into Sarah's van and Jake's car and

made their way across town to the Donahue apartment.

It was in a seedy, neglected part of the city, just on the fringes of a neighborhood known for its high crime rate.

"There's safety in numbers, right?" Molly muttered to Darby as they approached the address Shane had given them.

Darby gave Molly a withering look but didn't speak. She felt apprehensive too, but the fact that Shane had actually invited them over was a major breakthrough—one she wasn't going to miss.

The hallway to the apartment smelled of food cooking and stale cigarettes. The carpet was long overdue for a cleaning, and the walls needed a good coat of paint. The Donahue's door looked like all the others in the long, nondescript hallway. Inside, however, it was a different matter.

The tiny apartment was immaculately clean. The furniture, obviously secondhand, was arranged in a cozy fashion. Paintings, many of them signed with the signature "Shane D.," hung on the walls. Bread was baking in the oven and filling the room with a sweet, delicious smell.

"Shane, is that you?" A woman in faded blue jeans and a ragged men's T-shirt walked around the corner. She was drying a plate with a dish towel. She was slim and of medium height. Her hair, the same color as Shane's, was pulled away from her face in a barrette. It occurred to Darby that Shane's mother didn't look much older than Shane himself.

Her face registered surprise at the group with Shane.

"We're going to do some work here. That's all right, isn't it?"

"That would be just fine." Mrs. Donahue looked delighted. "Help yourself." She put the cup and towel down and moved into the center of the group. "Would you introduce me to your friends?"

Shane did so, giving a thumbnail sketch of each person in turn.

His mother behaved as though she couldn't have been more pleased to meet the Queen of England. When they were done, Mrs. Donahue backed toward what had to be a bedroom door. "I'll just get out of your way."

"You don't have to leave," Darby said.

"Thank you, but I should. You have things to do. Besides, I'm taking a night class at the junior college, and I have to study."

"Really? What are you taking?" Molly asked.

"It's an accounting class. Maybe someday I'll be a bookkeeper." Mrs. Donahue opened the door. There was a tiny, sparsely furnished bedroom on the other side. "Bye, kids. Come again."

"Okay," Izzy said enthusiastically. "Now, let's get on with it. Who could the graffiti culprits be? We know it has to be more than one person, maybe several, doing copycat work. If someone—the main guy or girl—got caught, I think most of the others would stop doing it. Copycats are doing it because it's popular, not because they have anything to say."

"So it's our job to find the core individual or gang," Jake concluded.

"How can we do that? We have no clues!"

"Yes we do," Shane said quietly.

"We do?" several people chimed. "What?"

"The graffiti itself. There are clues in the way it looks and what it says."

"Like what?" Andrew challenged.

"The south wall of the school was done by an *artist*. Someone with real talent. It looks more like a mural than like vandalism."

"True. Whoever did it is good," Andrew allowed.

"Which means we can narrow our field to people who have that kind of talent," Shane said. "Painters. The type of people who are in Brentwood's art classes or paint scenery and backdrops or promotional posters for the theater."

"We could get a list of every student in the school and start crossing off the nonartistic ones," Julie suggested. "We could even talk to teachers to find out who's a good doodler and who draws pictures on their books and in the margins of their papers."

"That would be me," Andrew said. "But I can hardly draw my breath, let alone a picture." He looked around the room. "It seems that *you* are quite an artist, Shane. I guess you'd be left on the list."

Shane was about to respond when Sarah interjected, "Andrew's right. There will be lots of innocent people on that list even after we cross out all the nonartists. What do we do about that?"

"Then we have to look at *what* is being written."

"The first sign of trouble was 'Killjoy was here.'

How's that supposed to help? This is going to be *hard*," Molly moaned.

" 'Killjoy' is a pretty good clue," Darby said. "How many people actually know the World War II story about 'Kilroy was here'?"

"Plenty. Everyone who's taken a history class, for example."

"We can find that out too. Not everyone takes a history class in ninth grade."

"Anyone who had a grandfather or great-grandfather in World War II might also know about Kilroy."

"Or anyone who watched a documentary on public television," Kate added grimly. "This is impossible."

"No it isn't." Shane's tone was determined. "We narrow the field person by person. We talk to teachers, get ideas. When we've got the list as short as we can make it, we'll check the names out one by one. According to Mr. Wentworth, the graffiti on the south wall was done early in the morning. The night janitor went home at four A.M. and the cooks found it when they arrived at six. Not many people could have alibis for four to six A.M. We'll just have to check it out."

"Call parents? Ask them if their kids were home in bed? Oh, come on, Shane! Get real!"

"We'll do what we have to," he retorted stubbornly. "Whatever it takes. Like *real* investigative reporters."

No one was willing to argue with Shane. He was showing genuine enthusiasm for the *Live!* projects. He'd invited them into his home. They would pursue this to its end as much for Shane as for the show.

At that moment, the doorbell rang. To everyone's surprise, Jason Danier was at the door.

Stamp out graffiti.

"Shane, I'm sorry I didn't call, but I had to tell someone—" Jason paused when he saw the room full of people staring at him. "You're busy. I'm sorry. I'll just . . ." His face fell and he started to turn away.

"Come here, you big dope." Shane grabbed him by the arm and pulled him inside. "You aren't interrupting anything. This is the *Live!* crew. We're brainstorming for a show we're putting together—the one on graffiti."

"Are you sure?" Jason fixed his gaze on Izzy.

"Yes. Maybe you can help us. A clear eye might be just what we need." Quickly Izzy explained their plan for ferreting out the graffiti artist.

A strange expression grew on Jason's face. When Izzy was done, Jason burst out laughing.

"It isn't *funny*," Kate protested.

"No, I don't suppose it is, but once you hear what I came to tell Shane, maybe you'll understand." Jason, when he smiled, was an entirely different person— handsome, appealing, warm.

"My art teacher has been on my back ever since I joined her class. She's always asking me to do special projects or 'samples' of my work. She never told me why until today. She's been showing my work to a man who wants to hire an artist!"

"And *you* are the artist?" Julie gasped. "Get outta here!"

"It's true. I was hired by the Brentwood Park Board to paint a mural on a wall in one of the parks! That's what struck me so funny. Some guy is running around painting for free and he's in trouble. I'm going to do the same thing and get paid!" Jason's eyes sparkled. "Good money too. You know that saying 'Crime doesn't pay'? Well, it's true. It sure doesn't pay like my new job will!"

The entire room erupted in happy congratulations. Mrs. Donahue even peeked out of the bedroom door to see what was going on. Jason beamed like a lighthouse, shaking hands and enduring congratulatory whacks on the back. Shane disappeared into the kitchen and reappeared with a liter of cola, which he promptly shook into a fizz and opened. It sprayed all over Jason and everyone laughed even more.

It was a new person who'd come to the door—a happy, excited, *employed* artist who was feeling really good about himself.

"Oh, I almost forgot," Jason said after they'd all settled down to more sodas and a bowl of popcorn Mrs. Donahue popped for the occasion. "There's more. You might be interested in adding this to your story about graffiti artists. "There's a man on the Park

Board who owns an avant-garde art studio near the park."

"What's 'avant-garde'?" Molly wanted to know.

"Underground, counterculture, innovative," Izzy said.

"Oh, you mean like the newest look or fashion?" Molly asked.

"Exactly. It's what's in, what's happening."

"Okay, now you can go on," Molly told Jason.

"He told me he wants to open his gallery to *street painters*!"

"Like the guy we're trying to catch?"

"Exactly. This man realizes that some street painters are really fine artists. He's done small showings of graffiti art in the past. Now, with all the publicity and uproar over the graffiti, he thinks it would be a good time to do a bigger show. It's something he's thought about for years."

"You mean somebody actually *likes* this stuff?" Kate sounded disbelieving.

"More than that. He's a *fan*. He wants to start a workshop for street painters. He's willing to open his large studio to them and provide them with canvasses. Cool, huh?"

"But why would he want to do this?" Andrew looked puzzled.

"He's very active in city government. He sees how upset the people have become about graffiti. It's his way of doing public service by getting the street painters off the streets."

"Won't that be expensive?"

"Not really. He'll have the painters stretch their

own canvasses. The studio is too large for him alone anyway. Besides, he's got a real soft spot in his heart for street painters. He says he likes their bold, free-wheeling style. He doesn't want taggers, of course. He thinks they are vandals too."

"Somebody actually likes graffiti?" Andrew was amazed.

"This man used to go to graffiti shows in New York in the '70s when he was an art student," Jason continued. His face glowed with delight. "The gallery director really believes that some of Brentwood's street artists have potential to work in the art field."

"What do you major in, vandalism?" Julie said sarcastically.

Even that didn't take the wind out of Jason's sails. "I've never told anyone this before, but I've always dreamed of being a graphic artist or sign painter. Now I think that someday maybe I could even be an art teacher. Finally, something is going my way!"

———

"I'm losing my mind!" Izzy complained as he moped around the media room. They'd just finished editing the material Izzy, Shane, and Gary had gathered at the Last Chance Ranch. That left Izzy's agile mind free to stew about the graffiti artist who was still on the loose.

"We've exhausted every possibility and we still can't pin it down. This guy can't just vanish into thin air!"

"He's been scared into stopping, though," Sarah

pointed out. "The 'artistic' graffiti hasn't shown up lately."

"True. That must mean the guy is a coward," Izzy deduced. "A sneaky little coward."

"You're just bent out of shape because you think that you should be able to figure out who 'Killjoy' is. Someone has out-witted you, and it's driving you nuts," Andrew said cheerfully.

"It's got to be logical," Izzy muttered. "And there's got to be a clue. Someone in this school is doing this, and we can't figure out who. We've been through everybody who can draw."

"Or even hold a pencil," Sarah added wearily.

"Everyone who took a history class that mentioned 'Kilroy,' and everyone who might, for some reason, be out very early in the morning. That leaves no one!"

"If it's not a likely suspect, then it's an unlikely one," Darby commented. "Maybe you're being too logical. Who's the least likely person to spray paint the walls at Brentwood?"

"Mr. Wentworth?" Josh suggested. "No one would ever suspect the administration of doing it. And he's probably old enough to have been in World War II."

"Wentworth . . . hmmm." Izzy put a finger to his chin and looked thoughtful.

"You can't believe I meant that!" Josh yelped.

"No, but you gave me an idea. Somebody totally unlikely. Somebody who might not have turned up on our lists."

"Who?" they all chimed.

"There's a little guy about three lockers down

from me. He never talks and he always keeps his eyes down. It just occurred to me that I've seen the inside of his locker when he changes books. He's a World War II buff. We talked about it once. He said he collected memorabilia. I noticed him because he had a picture of military generals inside his locker, and I thought it was weird."

Izzy glanced at his watch. "We've only got a couple minutes until the bell rings. Jake, Josh, Andrew, come with me. We've got to catch him while his locker is open. He's always quick to close it."

The guys disappeared in a rush.

"I hope they know what they're doing," Kate muttered.

"What *are* they doing?" Sarah asked.

"Confronting some poor little guy who likes toy soldiers, probably," Julie said.

Gary and Ms. Wright, who had been silently observing the goings-on, came to join the girls.

"Izzy's gotten a little carried away," Gary said. "Maybe I should convince him that we have enough on the graffiti story."

"Probably, if you can." Ms. Wright sighed. "He does tend to carry investigative news reporting a little too far."

Just then the guys returned with a squirming, red-faced, red-haired boy in tow. Izzy had him by the collar and dropped him neatly into a chair for interrogation.

"Spill it," Izzy ordered.

"I gotta go. I don't know what you're talking

about." The boy crossed his arms over his chest and glared at Izzy.

"We saw the wide markers and the spray-paint cans when you opened your locker to dump in your books. Why are they there?"

"I'm taking an art class. You got a problem with that?"

"You are not. We have a list of every art student in the school this semester."

"Maybe I took it *last* semester."

"We have that too."

Gary moved forward. "What's your name?" he asked softly.

The boy looked up. "Ralph. Ralph Wettinger."

"Well, Ralph, it looks as if these guys caught you with some suspicious stuff. Would you like to talk to us about it or do you prefer to go directly to the school office?"

"No!" Ralph's face flushed with panic. "I didn't do all that stuff. I'm not gonna get blamed for everything!"

Ralph was a lousy liar. When he realized what he'd just admitted, his shoulders sagged.

He squirmed in the chair for a while, picking at a hangnail on his thumb. When no one spoke and no one moved, Ralph decided to talk.

"Okay, so I spray painted a little on some walls. But I didn't do it all! I didn't do any of this ... garbage." His nose turned up. "Some creeps thought they were copying me, but they don't know how to do it! Now I'll get blamed for everything, and it's not all my fault!"

"Did you do the south wall of the school?" Gary asked.

Ralph's shoulders squared with pride. "Yeah. It's good too."

"No one said it wasn't, but it's not an appropriate place to draw. That's public property."

Ralph snorted. "Just look at the 'Kilroy' thing during the Second World War. That even got written up in history books. I was reading one that talked about it, and that's how I got the idea. I'd planned to just do it once or twice, but then some copycats thought it was funny and kept adding it to new places. Now there have to be dozens of people messing around with it."

Suddenly Ralph's shell of toughness crumbled, and the terror he was feeling showed in his face. "I started it, but I didn't wreck all those buses or walls. I don't want to be in trouble. What can I do?"

In an instant, he was transformed from a tough punk to a scared little boy. Ralph was very close to tears.

Rosie and Gary exchanged glances. "What you did wasn't right," Rosie said. "And you'll have to pay for the damage you've done. The rest will be up to the administration or the police."

Ralph turned sheet white.

"But I will go with you to the administration. Since we've been working on this story, I've become somewhat of an expert on graffiti. If you will confess to the initial vandalism, I will explain the copycat phenomenon. That's not going to prevent you from being punished, but there are others to blame as well, and you shouldn't have to take their punishment."

Ralph looked small and defeated in the chair. "It was never supposed to get like this. I just wanted to make my mark at school. Nobody even knows who I am." He shot a baleful glance at Izzy. "Except you. Now I'll probably get expelled."

"It's serious. There's no doubt about that. You've opened a real can of worms with this one." Ms. Wright was brutally honest.

Ralph looked up with terrified eyes. "As soon as the first copycat stuff happened, I realized what was going on. It just kept growing and growing, and I didn't know what to do. How do we get it to stop?"

How *would* they get it to stop? Graffiti painting was a private, sneaky sort of thing, done not only on immediately visible walls but also inside the stalls of bathrooms and on desks and school furniture. It was expensive and insidious and, as Ralph had pointed out, a real puzzle.

Everyone was silent. Ralph had opened a real Pandora's box with his spray paint and his "Killjoy was here."

Gary finally spoke. "Since we're doing the graffiti story anyway, I think it should be announced that 'Killjoy' has been apprehended and is being dealt with appropriately. Then go on to say that whoever else is caught defacing school property will be punished *very harshly*."

Ralph paled.

Gary continued, "I have a hunch that most of the nonsense will die down. Kids will lose interest quickly.

Only the dedicated will persist, and they'll have to be dealt with anyway."

"Maybe even that will be less of a problem if the street artists get their own studio," Izzy pointed out. He turned to Ralph, who was looking more remorseful by the minute. "If you'd had a studio to go to, a place you were welcome to paint, would you have gone?"

"Maybe," Ralph said. "I'd probably try it once, just to see what it was all about."

Ms. Wright tapped Ralph on the shoulder. "It's time to go."

"What's going to happen to me?" he asked weakly as he struggled to stand. His knees looked entirely too wobbly.

"I don't know. You should have thought of that before you started painting."

"But . . ."

"Responsibility. That's the name of the game," Ms. Wright said bluntly. "If you do something—either bad or good—then you'd better be prepared to take the consequences. Come on, Picasso, time to face the music."

———

Final taping was in progress. The story on the Last Chance Ranch and that of the graffiti artists would be aired together. Izzy's face flashed onto the screen.

"We have an update here at the *Live! From Brentwood High* news desk. There has been a decision made at the mayor's office *not* to regulate the sale of spray paint at this time. This news comes along with the announced opening of a 'Graffiti Gallery and Studio' at Fifth and Hargreaves next to the Flatbush Gallery. This studio is open to street artists. The mayor's office and gallery owner both hope that channeling this creative energy will be more effective than simply trying to enforce laws against vandalism.

"According to city sources, this approach seems to be working already. Since the apprehending of one major graffiti painter, others have begun to monitor themselves. With the Graffiti Gallery and Studio open and available, we should see a marked decrease in street painting soon.

"While there is no doubt, according to officials, that there will always be some problems with street artists and vandals, creative solutions such as these should make them more manageable."

Izzy looked directly into the camera and began to ad lib. Molly, at the teleprompter, began to panic as Izzy left the pre-planned script.

"If any of you street painters are out there, listen to me. What you're doing isn't worth it. If you want to 'express yourselves,' go to the gallery. It's a cool place and you won't be hassled. You don't want to lose the privileges you have. As you know from earlier in the show, I spent some time at the Last Chance Ranch. Trust me, you don't want your freedom taken away. Don't risk it. That's all for now, folks. Join us again next week at *Live! From Brentwood High.*"

Izzy folded his notes and leaned back in the chair with a huge sigh.

Josh pulled off his headphones and hung them on

the camera. "Great job, Izzy!" He waved to Julie who was watching the proceedings through the window. She disappeared, and when she returned she was carrying a big, lopsided but brightly frosted cake shaped like a television screen.

The rest of the *Live!* cast trailed in behind her, cheering.

"What's this about?" Izzy demanded.

"It's a celebration for our best show yet. It was Ms. Wright's idea," Molly said.

"Really?" Izzy turned to their instructor.

"Every time I think you kids can't do any better, you manage to pull it off anyway. I'm proud of all of you." Ms. Wright's voice crackled with emotion.

"Me too." Gary stepped into the circle of students. "I've been a lot of places and done a lot of things, but the energy you guys bring to these projects is incredible."

"Wow, compliments from teachers," Andrew said. "We must be good."

"Who baked the cake?" Izzy took a swipe of icing.

"Jake and Josh did it in the Home Ec. room," Darby said. "The oven rack was put in crooked so the cake's a little slanted, but it should taste fine."

Jake and Josh were getting a thorough ribbing for their culinary skills when Jason entered the media room. The party atmosphere evaporated at the look on his face.

"What's wrong?" Sarah asked, immediately wheeling her chair closer to him. "Are you sick?"

"Sort of. Sick inside." Jason sank onto a chair. His shoulders drooped and his hands hung limply between his knees. "I just found out that I'm moving."

"Moving? You just got here!" Izzy roared.

"My aunt and uncle want me to come to live with them in Alabama. They think I should have a 'fresh start.'"

"What's so bad about that?" Kate asked. "It sounds kind of nice, actually."

"When I left the ranch, I would have thought so too," Jason admitted. "I would never have believed that I might actually *like* it here." He looked up. "And if it weren't for some of you guys, I wouldn't have been happy. But you were friendly, and you acted like you cared."

He grinned crookedly at Izzy and Shane. "You even tried to 'walk in my shoes' at the Last Chance Ranch. Not many people would ever have done that. This is the first place I've been that people actually took time to try to understand me."

"And now, when we've finally figured you out, you're leaving," Shane summed it up abruptly. It was clear that he, too, was upset.

"When?"

"Two weeks. I'll have just enough time to complete the mural for the Park Board."

"So soon?" Izzy was shocked.

"The best thing about this is that I'll still get paid. I'm going to use the money to buy art supplies. My uncle said I could use the room over his garage as a studio."

"What are your aunt and uncle like?" Sarah asked softly. "Will you be happy there?"

"Probably. I know they'll be nice to me. He's a

preacher of some sort and is always trying to help kids get their lives straightened around." Jason stared at Sarah. "Do you think God is trying to tell me something in all of this?"

"It would be worth listening," she said with a smile. "Sometimes He uses pretty interesting situations to get His message across." She reached out and embraced Jason in a hug.

"God. Fresh starts. Who would have thought any of that could happen to me?" Slowly Jason moved around the room, shaking hands and hugging every one of the *Live!* staff. When he left the room, there were tears in his eyes. And in Izzy's. And in Shane's.

"This is too hard," Izzy said finally. "I get too emotionally involved. I'll never be a good news man."

"It's your passion that *makes* you good," Gary pointed out. He put a hand on Izzy's shoulder.

"I don't know. This particular show has meant a lot to me"—Izzy looked up—"and to Shane too. I can't think of anything that could ever top it—even if I wanted it to."

"Just wait," Gary advised. "There's something bigger and better right around the corner. You'll see."

————

When the staff of *Live! From Brentwood High* decides to do a feature on the lives of unwed teenage mothers who have kept their babies, everyone's eyes are opened. How does it feel to have to get a babysitter to go to class? Find out in *Faded Dreams*, book #6 in the LIVE! FROM BRENTWOOD HIGH series.

Turn the page for an exciting
Sneak Preview
of

The Suspect

Book #24 in the
CEDAR RIVER DAYDREAMS series
by Judy Baer

She was so sweet...
but could she be the thief?

The
Suspect

Judy Baer

Chapter One

"Have you heard the news?" Egg McNaughton's thin face glowed with excitement as he raced into the Hamburger Shack and skidded to a stop at a large table near the back of Cedar River's most popular high-school hangout.

Egg's sister, Binky, was close behind him. Her reddish brown hair practically stood on end and her eyes gleamed beneath pale lashes. "You'll never believe it! Never!"

Something momentous had obviously occurred.

Binky danced back and forth on her tiptoes like a spindly legged bird until Todd Winston reached out and grabbed her hand.

"Settle down and tell us what's up. We aren't mind readers."

"You're assuming they have *minds*. It's my guess that the McNaughtons have lost theirs entirely." Jennifer Golden tossed her blond hair away from her face and took a deep swig from the root beer mug in front of her. Egg and Binky were always excited about something. It was hard to take them seriously. Lexi Leighton and Peggy Madison burst out laughing.

Even the group at a neighboring table was drawn into Egg and Binky's exuberance. Minda Hannaford, Tressa and Gina Williams, Mary Beth Adamson, and Rita Leonard, all members of a clique of girls who called themselves the High Fives, were watching with growing interest.

Only Matt Windsor appeared to be actually listening to the agitated pair. "Quiet," he muttered. "Let them talk."

Matt, a dark, brooding boy who rarely smiled, actually grinned at Egg and Binky. "Ignore them," he advised.

"I'm glad *somebody* is taking us seriously," Egg said pompously. "And when you hear our news, you'll be sorry you didn't too." He glared at Jennifer accusingly.

"All right, what is it?" Jennifer rolled her eyes, sure that their news wasn't worth all this fuss.

"As you all know," Egg began importantly, "Binky and I are in marketing class this quarter."

"So? I'm in physics and I'm not bragging about it."

"That's because you're probably flunking it, Golden," Minda Hannaford sneered. A pouty blue-eyed blonde who always had a tart remark, Minda was not Jennifer's favorite person.

"Am not."

"Are too."

"Not."

"Too."

"Break it up," Egg ordered. "You're not paying attention."

Minda and Jennifer glared at each other but turned toward Egg.

He cleared his throat. "Binky and I have been named class managers of the *School Store!*"

There was a moment of startled silence at both tables. The School Store was a small retail operation run by the marketing class as a hands-on learning opportunity. The store sold school supplies, sweat shirts, running suits, even jackets with the Cedar River logo emblazoned on them. At Christmastime the store usually did a brisk gift business selling stuffed animals and affordable trinkets to impoverished high-school students. It was also a popular hangout between classes because two years earlier the enterprising marketing class had installed an iced cappuccino maker and gained permission from the school administration to sell it during the lunch hour. Being selected to be manager of the School Store was the equivalent of being chosen class president or Student Council member. Those spots usually went to the brightest and most organized students.

"You two? Get outta here!" Minda was the first to express the doubt and amazement that everyone felt. "I thought they had accounting brains do that."

"Are you saying I'm *not* an accounting brain?" Egg asked huffily.

"You're more of a *bird* brain, McNaughton," Tressa said.

The High Fives cackled at her humor. They were a tight-knit group, bound by loyalty to one another. Even if Tressa's statement *hadn't* contained the least bit of humor, they all would have laughed. Becoming a member of the elite club of girls wasn't easy. Lexi had learned that hard lesson when she first moved to Cedar River. When she had rejected their rite of initiation, she had made more enemies than friends in the group.

Egg was blustering a retort to Tressa when Matt spoke. "I don't think I've ever set foot in the School Store."

Everyone stared at him in amazement. "Where have *you* been?"

Matt shrugged. "Around. But I'm not crazy about school. Why would I want to *shop* there?"

"Matt's right," Rita said. "Who wants a bunch of goofy clothes with 'Cedar River High' written all over them?"

"I do!" Binky said. "There are great things in the store. Cheap too."

"It *is* a school tradition," Lexi pointed out. "When I moved to Cedar River I asked someone about the store. I was told that it's been a part of the school for nearly twenty years, ever since they started the marketing program. It's where the marketing students get to practice what they learn in the classroom."

"Exactly!" Egg agreed. "We're involved in every aspect of running the store. We make the displays, keep the books and deposit the money, handle the customers—"

"And we get to go on a buying trip!" Binky interjected enthusiastically.

"What do you need to buy if you already work at the store?" Rita asked.

"The stuff we'll sell, of course. Our class has already decided to put in a line of cards and stationery. We get to pick them out."

"Get something funny," Todd advised. "And something for parents. I almost forgot my mom's birthday this year. It would have been great if I could have found a card at the School Store."

"Good idea." Egg whipped a tiny notebook out of his pocket and scribbled a note. "We want our customers to be happy."

"I can guess what we'll be hearing about for the rest of the month," Jennifer groaned.

Egg ignored her. "We have almost five hundred dollars to spend on our buying trip, so suggestions for things you'd like to see in the store are welcome."

"Five hundred dollars?" Mary Beth Adamson had been the quietest of the High Fives until now. Her eyes grew round with surprise. "That's a lot of money!"

"I told you that you'd be impressed!" Egg said, his expression one of smug satisfaction.

"Who works for you? In the store, I mean." Mary Beth was paying close attention now.

"Students. The people we hire. The marketing students do the big stuff, but regular students can come in for an interview and be hired to work during their free hour. We're going to be open longer hours this year. We'll open before school starts and close half an hour after the last bell. Marketing students work there once or twice a month during marketing class as well. We'll train our employees and oversee their work."

"Cool," Mary Beth said.

"You should come and apply," Egg suggested importantly. "After all, you know the manager."

"I'm a manager too," Binky pointed out, tired of having Egg take all the glory for their new venture.

Egg scowled at her, annoyed that she'd try to take the wind from his sails.

"Well, I *am*!"

Hoping to diffuse the inevitable fight the McNaughtons would have if this conversation was allowed to continue, Lexi hurried to ask, "How were you two chosen to be managers?"

"Because they're the best for the job, of course!" Angela Hardy beamed at Egg and Binky as if they'd just successfully completed a moon landing or delicate brain surgery. Egg's response was a goofy, smitten grin. Angela was a slender, dark-haired girl with smooth, clear skin. She was quite beautiful when she smiled.

Egg and Angela had been dating since Angela came to Cedar River. She'd had a bumpy beginning here, first being homeless, then living with her mother at the city mission. Egg's initial curiosity about Angela and her homelessness had caused him to spend a night on the streets trying to comprehend what it might be like. Somehow, that strange and not-too-wise decision had created a bond between them that had grown even stronger over time.

Things had steadily improved for the Hardys since then. Now they had their own apartment, and Angela's mother had a job she could support them with. Egg had been Angela's enthusiastic champion through those dark days, and Angela had never forgotten his kindness. What's more, the gang agreed that they made a perfect—if unlikely—couple.

Angela scrambled out of her seat to fling her arms around Binky and Egg. Her arms lingered around his waist, and he seemed unwilling to drop his hand from her shoulder. It wasn't until Tressa and the rest of the eavesdropping High Fives started to make kissy noises on the backs of their hands that Angela stepped out of his embrace.

Uncharacteristically, Egg was not embarrassed by the teasing. The appointment as School Store manager had already given him newfound confidence.

"I think we should congratulate our friends," Todd suggested, "and buy them a burger to celebrate."

"I'm not *that* happy," Minda huffed and turned back to her own table. Tressa, Gina, Rita, and Mary Beth followed.

"Ignore them," Peggy Madison advised. *"We'll* buy."

Egg and Binky maneuvered two more chairs around the table. As Egg sat down, Binky threw her arms around him and gave him a noisy smack on the cheek.

"What was that about?" Jennifer wondered. "You *kissed* your brother! Yuk."

"I couldn't help it. I'm just so excited about the store. Isn't it the greatest news you've ever heard?"

"I didn't know you and Egg were so interested in retail merchandising," Peggy said.

"We're not. Or, at least, we weren't—until now. When you get picked for something special you can't help being excited." Binky glowed like a little lantern.

Egg and Binky, while two of the sweetest, funniest students in the school, were not necessarily the most popular. Their quirkiness and Egg's gangly bean-pole appearance had always set them apart. This was a notable moment for the McNaughtons.

As might be expected, their friends were still a little doubtful about this honor.

"How many people were considered for management?" Jennifer inquired.

Lexi shot her a warning glance.

Jennifer was trying to discover if Egg and Binky had had competition or if they'd become managers by default. She shrugged when she caught Lexi's stern look. *Can I help it if I'm curious?* her expression said.

Fortunately Egg and Binky didn't catch on. "Several people," Binky said. "Our teacher and advisor Mr. Kahler said . . . Look! There he is now!"

Mr. Walter Kahler had entered the Hamburger Shack and was winding his way through the crowded tables to the back of the room like a man with a purpose. He stopped when he reached their table.

"Edward, Bonita, I'd like to talk with you for a moment."

Todd blinked. Lexi and Peggy shifted in their chairs. Jennifer covered her mouth to hide a smile. None of them were used to hearing Egg and Binky called by their real names.

"I have some catalogs in my car I'd like you to take a look at. I want you to be familiar with the kinds of items you'll be seeing at the market when we go on our buying trip for the store. I meant to give them to you at school today, but I was called to the office last hour and missed you. Can you take them home and scan them tonight?"

"Sure." Egg jumped to his feet and Binky followed. "We'll get them out of your car."

"Hi, Mr. Kahler," Minda said. She and her friends had watched this exchange with rapt interest.

"Hello, Minda. We've missed you in accounting class this quarter."

"I don't want you to be offended, Mr. Kahler," Minda began, "but are you sure you've made the right choice for store managers?"

Lexi swung around in her seat and stared at Minda. How *dare* she. . . .

But Mr. Kahler did not interpret the question as an insult at all.

"Positive. Mr. and Miss McNaughton will be excellent. They have the drive, the determination, the energy. . . ."

"They do have that, all right," Todd agreed. "Egg and Binky have more energy than any other people I know."

"Exactly. And their enthusiasm is contagious. I think they'll be the right combination to make the store work. We've got a lot of changes planned for the future, and I believe Edward and Bonita are the ones to implement them. I'm looking forward to a good experience."

After Mr. Kahler left, the kids stared at one another in amazement.

"Was he talking about the same people we know?" Jennifer asked in surprise. "Maybe there's another Edward and Bonita that we haven't met."

"Very funny," Angela huffed. "They'll be great. Why don't you believe in them?"

"We do believe in them. It's just that we didn't know anyone else did!" Jennifer skewered Angela with a gaze. "They are a little quirky, you know."

Angela laughed. "I know. But I also know they can make this work. I'm happy for them."

"Me too," said someone from the adjoining booth. Amazingly, the statement had come out the mouth of Minda Hannaford.

Minda was usually Egg's worst tormentor. She never missed an opportunity to tease him relentlessly. What made it so much worse was that for a long time Egg had had a hopeless crush on Minda.

When Angela had appeared on the scene and Egg had transferred his love interest to her, Minda had been strangely upset. She didn't want Egg herself, but she wasn't accustomed to being rejected by him either.

"*You're* glad? Why?" Jennifer was painfully blunt.

"Maybe Egg and Binky will need a fashion buyer. After all, they don't have any sense of style. I'd hate to see them spend money on stupid sweat shirts. They need something in the store with *style*. And since I am the fashion columnist for the *Cedar River Review*, maybe I can help." Minda referred to the school newspaper which several of them worked on.

"I've got some great ideas for awesome new sweats and jackets."

"What makes you think Egg would ask for your help?"

Minda ignored Jennifer. "I wish everything in the

School Store didn't have to have that stupid logo on it."

"Merchandise has to carry the school logo. It's a store rule. We're not supposed to compete with local businesses."

"I'd never wear a bathing suit with that logo on it," Minda said derisively. "Egg and Binky had better be careful what they order, that's all I can say." She stood, and the rest of the High Fives rose with her. "Let's get out of here."

Obediently, the other girls followed.

"She sure leads them around," Peggy commented after they'd disappeared through the door of the Shack.

"And they let her. It's surprising. The only one I'd expect that of is Mary Beth Adamson," Angela commented. "She's very quiet and seems different from the others. The rest should be able to hold their own with Minda."

"We've talked enough about them," Todd said. "What do you think about Egg and Binky's news?"

"It's great, but . . ."

"We all know what you mean, Angela," Lexi assured her. "Egg and Binky are the best, but sometimes things do turn out . . . oddly . . . for them."

"I hope they know what they're doing," Peggy said quietly. "After all, the School Store has a pretty big budget. I hope they don't break the bank."

Cedar River Daydreams

1 ▪ New Girl in Town
2 ▪ Trouble with a Capital "T"
3 ▪ Jennifer's Secret
4 ▪ Journey to Nowhere
5 ▪ Broken Promises
6 ▪ The Intruder
7 ▪ Silent Tears No More
8 ▪ Fill My Empty Heart
9 ▪ Yesterday's Dream
10 ▪ Tomorrow's Promise
11 ▪ Something Old, Something New
12 ▪ Vanishing Star
13 ▪ No Turning Back
14 ▪ Second Chance
15 ▪ Lost and Found
16 ▪ Unheard Voices
17 ▪ Lonely Girl
18 ▪ More Than Friends
19 ▪ Never Too Late
20 ▪ The Discovery
21 ▪ A Special Kind of Love
22 ▪ Three's a Crowd
23 ▪ Silent Thief
24 ▪ The Suspect

Other Books by Judy Baer

▪ Paige
▪ Adrienne
▪ Dear Judy, What's It Like at Your House?
▪ Dear Judy, Did You Ever Like a Boy
  (who didn't like you?)

9605

A Note From Judy

I'm glad you're reading LIVE! FROM BRENTWOOD HIGH! I hope I've given you something to think about as well as a story to entertain you. If you feel you have any of the problems that Darby and her friends experience, I encourage you to talk with your parents, a pastor, or a trusted adult friend. There are many people who care about you!

I love to hear from my readers, so if you'd like to receive my newsletter and a bookmark, please send a self-addressed, stamped envelope to:

Judy Baer
Bethany House Publishers
11300 Hampshire Avenue South
Minneapolis, MN 55438

Be sure to watch for my *Dear Judy* . . . books at your local bookstore. These books are full of questions that you, my readers, have asked in your letters, along with my response. Just about every topic is covered—from dating and romance to friendships and parents. Hope to hear from you soon!

Dear Judy, What's It Like at Your House?
Dear Judy, Did You Ever Like a Boy
   (who didn't like you?)

Teen Series From
Bethany House Publishers

Early Teen Fiction (11–14)

HIGH HURDLES by Lauraine Snelling
Show jumper DJ Randall strives to defy the odds and achieve her dream of winning Olympic Gold.

SUMMERHILL SECRETS by Beverly Lewis
Fun-loving Merry Hanson encounters mystery and excitement in Pennsylvania's Amish country.

THE TIME NAVIGATORS by Gilbert Morris
Travel back in time with Danny and Dixie as they explore unforgettable moments in history.

Young Adult Fiction (12 and up)

CEDAR RIVER DAYDREAMS by Judy Baer
Experience the challenges and excitement of high school life with Lexi Leighton and her friends—over one million books sold!

GOLDEN FILLY SERIES by Lauraine Snelling
Readers are in for an exhilarating ride as Tricia Evanston races to become the first female jockey to win the sought-after Triple Crown.

JENNIE MCGRADY MYSTERIES by Patricia Rushford
A contemporary Nancy Drew, Jennie McGrady's sleuthing talents promise to keep readers on the edge of their seats.

LIVE! FROM BRENTWOOD HIGH by Judy Baer
When eight teenagers invade the newsroom, the result is an action-packed teen-run news show exploring the love, laughter, and tears of high school life.

THE SPECTRUM CHRONICLES by Thomas Locke
Adventure and romance await readers in this fantasy series set in another place and time.

SPRINGSONG BOOKS by various authors
Compelling love stories and contemporary themes promise to capture the hearts of readers.

WHITE DOVE ROMANCES by Yvonne Lehman
Romance, suspense, and fast-paced action for teens committed to finding pure love.